THREE
MILES
PAST

THREE
MILES
PAST

THREE MILES PAST

Stories

Stephen Graham Jones

OPEN ROAD

INTEGRATED MEDIA
NEW YORK

"No Takebacks" originally appeared in *Phantasmagorium* Issue 1 (2011)

ISBN: 978-1-5040-9632-4

This edition published in 2024 by Open Road Integrated Media, Inc.
180 Maiden Lane
New York, NY 10038
www.openroadmedia.com

for Randy Howard, for everything

and for William Colton Hughes

CONTENTS

Interstate Love Affair   3
No Takebacks   59
The Coming of Night   99

Story Notes   145
Acknowledgments   157
About the Author   159

CONTENTS

When Hippocrates visited the 'mad Democritus' in Abders, he found him sitting in front of his house surrounded by dead, disemboweled birds. He was writing a treatise on insanity and was dissecting the birds in order to localize the . . . source of madness.

—Mikhail Bakhtin

My head is full of monsters and I'm one of them.

—Richard Kadrey

INTERSTATE LOVE AFFAIR

THE DERIDDER ROADKILL

Unidentified, controversial remains discovered on the side of Highway 12 just outside Deridder, Louisiana in 1996, and subsequently either lost or taken. According to The Dequincy News, the remains expressed both canine and primate characteristics. The photographs support this. For many, the Deridder Roadkill established that the Cajun werewolf (loupgarou) wasn't just legend. For others, the roadkill was a skunk-ape, or chupacabra, even a misplaced baboon. To the Louisiana Department of Wildlife and Fisheries, the photographs are just morbid documentation of a large, brown Pomeranian dog.

That's one explanation.

1.

William drank three beers in his truck in the parking lot, just to get ready. He lined the cans up on the dash, looked through the second and third at the metal front door of the pound. The animal control trucks were nosed up to the building; it was almost five o'clock. William peeled the tab off a fourth beer, looked into it and shook his head no, because he knew he shouldn't. Four was too many. He told himself not to be stupid. That there was no room for error. And then he laughed, killed the beer.

The fifth and sixth were nothing, not after four, but then, balancing the sixth on the dash like a wall, William straightened his legs against the floorboard, pushing himself back into the seat: for a moment the cans had quit being cans, had become the cushions him and his brother used to build forts with in the living room.

William hit himself in the side of the head until he was sure he wasn't going to cry. He used a baby wipe from the glove compartment to stop the bleeding. Most people don't know about baby wipes. William held the wet paper—fabric, almost—to his temple. It was cool, perfect. Then he held it over his mouth, breathed through it until he could breathe evenly again.

The fourth beer was a mistake, he knew that now, but it was too late. It had to be today.

Instead of leaving the cans on his dash, he dropped them over his shoulder, through the sliding rear glass. They landed in the bed. Any sound they made was muffled by the fiberglass camper shell. But they didn't make any noise.

William stepped down from the front seat and was almost to the wheelchair ramp of the pound when he had to go back, check to see if he'd locked the door of the truck. And then, just because he was there, he checked the passenger door too, and its vent window, and then the handle on the camper, then the camper itself.

If he put his hands around his eyes, his nose to the black glass, he could see the silver cans in the bed of the truck, and if he looked into the cab, there were the classifieds, still open to Pets, four of the ads circled in blue, but he couldn't spend all day in the parking lot.

The same way William knew about baby wipes, he knew about this.

He smiled and stepped away from the glass, faking a shrug for anybody watching, as if he'd just settled something with himself. There was nobody out there to see him. Just the same number of cars and animal control trucks there had been when he first pulled up.

It was time.

He nodded to himself, moving his neck the way he imagined someone with the last name Pinzer would, then remembered to keep the tips of his fingers in the tops of his pants pockets. Because if he didn't, the pound attendant would keep looking at his hands, at William's hands, and then William would start looking down to them too, until that was all he could do.

Smile, he said to himself. People trust an easy face.

He hooked the door open with his forearm, caught it with his shoulder, stepped in sideways.

It was the usual waiting room—cast-off chairs, metal tables salvaged from the county's overflow warehouse. The lamp was one that an attendant's mothers had probably given them years ago, when she was updating her sitting room. The too-green plant would be from another attendant, who had pretended she'd bought it with the coffee money but had really paid for it herself, to liven the place up, keep her from slitting her wrists one night.

William took it all in in a dismissive glance, noticed that his hand was in his beard.

He lowered it slowly, his teeth set with the effort.

Behind the desk, nobody. On the wall, certificates, awards, letters of thanks framed twenty years ago. Near the hall leading back to the barking, two clipboards. One from today, Monday, and one for the weekend.

William swallowed, leaned toward the lists.

The dog column for the weekend had thirty-nine dogs, each identified first by location, then tag, if there was one, then just description: *25–30lbs., black, white tail-tip. Probably Lab, Lab-mix.* The dead, the run over, the already burned in the incinerator.

William smiled, found his hand covering his mouth again, made it go back down.

The girl who opened the door beside the lists stopped, pulled her breath in sharp, had to crane her head back to see all the way up to William's face.

William opened his mouth, stepped back, holding his hands up to show, to show her—

She was looking to the metal door in the waiting room now, though. Then back up to William. "It was open?" she said, crinkling the corners of her eyes about how that shouldn't have been the case.

William nodded. She was twenty-three maybe, a rich caramel color, silver chain around her neck, holding a pink stone to the hollow of her throat. Otherwise, she was a nurse: green scrubs, yellow rubber gloves. Hair pulled back. It made her eyes better.

Hands, William said to himself.

They went back to their pockets, and he could tell from the way the caramel girl's features softened that this was better. That what his hands in his pockets did to his shoulders, how they were round now, making him look stooped, embarrassed of his height—a lifetime of standing in the back row, a thousand old ladies asking for help with the top shelf—that he wasn't a scary man in a flannel jacket anymore. Just William. Bill, Bill Pinzer.

The girl nodded to the list with her mouth.

"Any luck?" she said.

William knew to pause before answering, and then not to answer anyway, just shake his head no.

The girl was looking at the door again.

"We close at five, y'know?"

"Sorry," William said, looking over her shoulder at the wire glass in the door behind her. As if looking for his dog. ". . . I just—my work. Five. You know."

The girl looked at him for maybe four seconds, then shrugged.

"Thad was supposed to lock the door," she said, finally. "Not your fault."

William nodded.

"You seen him up here?" the girl asked.

"Ted?"

"Thad—don't worry. Listen. Your pet, sir. When did it—"

"Saturday."

The girl turned to the door, zipping her keys out from her belt, towards the lock. William felt his lungs burning with air, made himself breathe, breathe.

"What kind?" she asked, not looking at him.

"Not sure," William said, shrugging in case she could see his reflection somewhere. "I only got him last week."

The girl opened the door, turned up to William.

"This is an adult dog?"

"Yeah, yes."

"Did you check the prior owner?"

William nodded. When the girl gave the door to him, she flipped it a bit so they weren't quite touching it at the same time. Like it would conduct something between them. Something more than she wanted. William's lips thinned behind his beard but he closed his eyes, stepped, stepped again, until it became a walk.

"Color, then?"

"Kind of . . . brownish. Black maybe. I'll know him."

"Husky, Bull, Lab?"

"I don't—you want me to call my friend?"

The girl looked back to William, stopped in the hall, as if to go back to the front desk, and then she looked ahead of them too. William could see it in her eyes: it was already past five, right?

"Maybe you'll see him," she said, turning around again.

She came up maybe to William's sternum.

At the first corner she palmed the radio she had on her belt, said into it that she was taking a gentlemen back into "Large Dogs." William watched her thumb the radio back off, hook it to its plastic clip.

"Thad?" he said.

The girl nodded, shrugged like she was sorry.

William shook his head no, though. "It's good you do that," he said.

"We had something happen—it's nothing. Couple of years ago. Listen. We're going to go through the forty-pounders first, all right?"

William nodded, took the next corner with her.

Two years, then. It had already been two years.

Every few steps there was a drain, and every forty feet, maybe, a twenty-foot hose coiled on the concrete wall.

The first dog they got to exploded against his chain-link, his saliva going arm over arm down the metal.

The girl held her hand out—this one?

William shook his head no without even looking again, and they went on, run after run, until they came to an obviously pregnant dog. Mastiff, maybe, two generations back.

"That her?" the girl asked.

William hesitated a moment before shaking his head no.

"She's going to have puppies," he said.

The girl shook her head no, shrugged like an apology. One with calluses on it.

William looked to her for an explanation.

"We'll—our doctor . . ." She was searching for words, falling back on what sounded like a pamphlet: "Any stray we release, we fix, right?"

William nodded, looked to the bitch again. Got it: "So I can't have her?"

"Not today," the girl said, looking at the dog too, then away, as if she had to. "After the procedure, though . . ."

"I should find Lobo first," William said, remembering.

The girl zipped her keys out, a nervous thing, and they moved on. Lobo was four runs down, a large Rottweiler with scarred eyebrows.

William smiled, wrapped his fingers around the chain link, and dropped to his knees.

The dog crashed into the fence then fell back onto his hind legs. They collapsed under him. Bad hips.

"Nothing to do about that, is there?" he said.

"Acetaminophen for the pain," the girl said. "You're sure that's him, though?"

Because of the snarling, the snapping.

William shrugged, squinched one side of his face up.

"I didn't—my friend. I shouldn't even tell you this. He doesn't know I have him, Lobo."

"You *stole* him?"

William closed his eyes, as if controlling his voice.

"He kept him chained to a telephone pole all day." He shrugged. "Not even shade, y'know? The kids after school, I'd see them . . . Doesn't matter."

The girl was watching the dog now. Again.

"So Lobo's not his name?"

"It's his new name."

The girl didn't smile, didn't nod, just looked to the dog, on one side of the wire door, William on his knees on the other.

"I—I . . ." she started, then pulled the radio back to her mouth, thumbed it open, but finally didn't say anything.

"What already?" Thad snapped back, in the middle of what sounded like a bad scene with a large cat.

Instead of reporting, the girl smiled over her hand. At William.

William smiled back.

"Nothing," she said, lowering the radio back to her belt. "This isn't procedure, you know that, right?" she said.

William shrugged. "Don't want to get you in trouble," he said, reaching back, touching his wallet.

The girl shook her head no.

"It has to cost something," William said.

"Twenty-five," the girl said, taking down the rainbow leash from its hook by 24B, Lobo's run. "If there was going to be any paperwork, I mean," she added. "Twenty-five for shots and neuter."

William nodded, watching her.

"If there was going to be paperwork," he repeated.

She nodded with him, watching Lobo.

"Not like I'm on the clock anymore, really," she said, shrugging, passing the leash over. "Right?"

William worked the clasp on the leash, the skin on the side of his index finger alive where it had brushed her hand.

Behind the chain-link, Lobo was growling now, just a steady rumble.

"Thanks," William said.

The girl smiled. "For what? I'm not even here, right?"

William didn't let himself smile, then stood in the door of the run with her when she opened it. Like, if Lobo had anything bad, any violence he'd been saving up for the last thirty-six hours, William was going to be the one to take it here.

He was an old dog with bad hips, though. Used to being the biggest, sure, his head a cinderblock he could clear a room with. But William had been doing this for years, from Florida to Texas. All along I-10.

When the dog slung his head around, William popped his knee to the side, rattling its teeth, then, covering it with his flannel body, he popped the dog once with the heel of his hand, hard, at the base of his spine. Just enough for the back legs to give. Then it was just a matter of leaning down onto the thick neck, working the rainbow leash around, clasping it to itself.

The dog's—*Lobo's*—eyes shot red almost immediately with

the pressure, the lack of air, and William kept his hand close to the clasp, so he had to walk hunched over.

The girl was on the other side of the hall now, a can of something defensive in her hand.

William smiled.

"Not his fault," he said, urging the dog along.

"He won't—he won't get out again. . . ?"

"The fence—" William said, making more of the struggle than there was, "fixed, yeah . . . don't worry," and then left the girl there like that, never even had to use the Pinzer name, or Pinker, or whatever the hell it had been.

Two dogs later—a Shepherd-mix and a Golden Retriever, each from the classifieds, families he'd had to make earnest, shuffling promises to—William pulled into a gas station, checked all his doors, and asked the clerk for the bathroom key.

"Have to buy something," the clerk said, shrugging that it wasn't his rule, but hey.

William looked down the candy aisle behind him, came back to the clerk.

"I will," he said.

"*First,*" the clerk added.

He was five-eight, maybe. A smoker.

William stared at him, stared at him, then lifted an air freshener off the revolving display by the register. Ninety-nine cents. He laid down a dollar, counted out one nickel and two pennies.

"Bag?" the clerk asked.

William shook his head no.

The air freshener was an ice cream cone, pink. It smelled like bubble gum. William tucked it into the chest pocket of his flannel jacket and took the key the clerk held across the counter. It was chained to the rusted steel rim of a go-cart, maybe. Or a kid's old three-wheeler. Nine inches across, four-hole, maybe eight pounds.

William held it easy, nodded to the clerk, and chanced a look out to his truck. It was parked against the shattered payphone.

No plates visible, just a side shot, a profile. Hardly even a real color.

William stepped away from the security camera, rounded the corner of the building for the bathroom. When the door wouldn't lock behind him, he set the key with its ATV rim down on the concrete, as a doorstop. And then he unrolled his leather case, let the water run until it was hot, and started applying the razor to his face, to his beard.

Because the door wasn't shut all the way, the mirror didn't steam up. William took note of this. Mirrors were always a problem. Scratched in this one were years of names and profanity and lopsided shapes—stars, crosses, lines that were going to be something complicated but got interrupted when the door had opened.

Something complicated: William smiled, pulled the skin tight against his jaw, his six-week beard collecting in the drain, then froze, his elbow out like a bat wing.

A noise, at the door?

In the mirror, William was distant, his face lathered in the pink soap from the dispenser. Distant but coiled.

It was nothing. Raccoon nosing the base of the closed door. Blowby from the big trucks.

William returned to his beard, stopping with just a mustache for a bit—his father's, silver the farther it got from his mouth—then going fast over it, deep enough that, near the lip on the left side, the razor burn he could already feel welled up into tiny points of blood. Like he was sweating it.

Outside, a car or truck rolled across the hose attached to the bell.

Past that, the interstate, its steel-belted hum.

William closed his eyes, let it wash over him, then slammed his open hand into the side of the sink, told himself he wasn't alone, that this could have been it—that you can't do that, close your eyes in public places. Alone, maybe. But even then.

William rolled the razor back into its pack, tied the string and ran the water until his beard was gone, and then he peed on top of it. Because the urine, leeching through whatever the hair was going to ball up against in the pipes, the urine would corrode the hair into something else.

After the beard, William took his shirt off, held it up to the light over the mirror. It was clean, so he didn't burn it, but he didn't put it back on, either. Just the jacket. Driving at night was better with no shirt. And he was going to make Beaumont by dawn.

First, though, the clerk.

William picked up the key and its ATV wheel, his middle finger in the groove where the wheel had been welded together. So it would roll off when he threw it, the key slinging around it on the chain like a fast, tiny moon.

The car that had pulled up to the gas tanks was a Chevette. Kids, one of them standing at the rear bumper. William looked down, away from any eye contact, then walked far enough around the side of the building to lift the wheel behind him like a bowling ball, like a disc. But then the kid was calling something out to him.

William turned to him.

The kid hooked his head into the gas station.

"He said I'm next."

William looked through the unbroken plate glass, to the small image of himself on the security monitor, and nodded, held the key up, showing he was surrendering it. The kid started across the slick concrete to take it. His arm was covered in blue tattoos. William took a half step back then set the wheel with its key down on the curb, and he was already walking away, already disappearing.

His truck was a 1981 F-250, and it was legal: stickers, registration, insurance. Each light worked, except the cargo. The wire that fed it was tied into the dome light, inside the cab, just over the back window. To get it to work—the cargo—William just had to take the plastic case off the dome light, pull the bulb, and set the raw wire into the socket, work the bulb in with it like a fuse.

He was forty-two miles from the gas station when he started working the plastic bubble off. It was cold, stiff, would break easy if he wasn't careful, then everybody would see the bare bulb, know something was wrong. He couldn't heat it up with the light though, either; if you were driving with your dome on, the state cops had to assume it was to find another beer, or to see the nudie mag on your passenger seat. So William edged the plastic bubble out one corner at a time with his right hand, his left steady on the wheel, and had been seeing it for maybe two seconds before it registered: a dark lump, stretched out along the shoulder of the interstate.

He smiled, forgot the dome light. Replayed the dark lump in his head.

When his rearview was clear he eased over, then turned his lights off and backed up twenty yards at a time, letting the tractor trailers sweep past. If they saw him, none of them blew their horns, though something did move in the grass once, which could have been a bottle, whipped out the passenger side at seventy miles per hour, the way the truckers liked to do it. William knew this from his father, had learned it at ten years old, how to sit perfectly still every few miles, his back pressing into the seat, a wine cooler bottle spinning past his face, connecting with a mile marker, his father watching in the side mirror then slamming the heel of his hand into the top of the wheel in celebration.

William never thought about it on purpose, but sometimes it came unbidden, all on its own. Not the bottles so much as the high-up seat, how still he had to sit in it, how he had to push on the legs of his jeans to stay like that long enough for the bottle to slice by his face. And how, even though he didn't want to, he'd listen along with his dad, for the chance of shattering glass behind them.

Sometimes, ten years old again, he would be in the seat listening, and other times he would be in the ditch, waiting for the bottle to slam into his head.

He was in the truck now, though. *His* truck.

It was important to always remember that.

He stopped alongside the dark lump and watched it for long minutes. The way none of the people driving by even noticed it.

He nodded that the world was a good place, a good place for someone like him, then opened his door, the dome light sputtering, the bulb half-out. He reached back in, tapped it into place, the current running through him to the ground for an instant. It was nothing.

He approached from downwind, to get the smell, know the whole animal, the blood, the feces, the fear if there'd been any, if it had looked up into the headlights. Because of the slant of the ditch he had to go on three points—both feet and one hand, the other shielding his eyes from the traffic.

Driving by, he'd thought it was a deer, maybe, its coat matted with blood, making it black, but now, now it was a dog, just too big.

He made himself move slow, just walk.

From his truck, no barking. Night falling down all around him.

He stepped up onto the shoulder and already there was blood. Just spatter, like a mist that had settled. He stepped around it as best he could, caught an airhorn for his effort. It straightened his back, took his breath in the best possible way.

And then he smiled an accidental smile: a *bear*. A little black, a cub maybe. That was what it was.

William lowered himself to it, running his hand along its thick coat.

A bear.

He had never touched one before.

Its shoulder and head were shattered, one of its forelegs missing, burned off on the asphalt. But a *bear*. William could feel himself getting hard in his pants, looked to the interstate just in time for a dummy light to blaze across his face.

The hand he'd had at his crotch came up to his eyes.

The cop walked up out of the light, his hand to the butt of his pistol, his flashlight feeling out through the ditch, splashing against William's truck.

William stayed with the bear. Just touching it.

"What you got?" the cop said.

William shrugged, almost said *Billy Pinzer* but instead just watched a cab-over like his father's push past. Pulling silage, it smelled like.

What he had to do now was breathe evenly. Not run. Remember to swallow.

The cop eased around the bear so he was facing traffic, played his light across the bear, then up to William again.

"You hit it?" he asked.

William shook his head no. "Just saw it, I guess."

The cop kind of laughed. "And you—you *stopped*?"

William shrugged. "Thought it might be . . . you know. Hurt."

The cop didn't nod but didn't quite keep his head still either. He trained the light down onto the bear again.

"Probably endangered," he said. "You want it, that it? The skin, teeth, that shit?"

William shook his head no, stood.

"What'll—what'll happen to it?" he said.

The cop watched a pair of headlights long enough that William turned. They were bouncing off the yellow line. The cop exhaled through his nose.

"Can't leave it here," he said. "Buzzards'll come, and—shit. They're endangered too, yeah?"

William pretended to suppress a disgusted laugh.

"I'll call it in maybe," the cop said. "Biologists like this kind of shit. Hell if I know why."

William nodded, made himself keep not looking to his truck. The cop was, though. His light was already playing on the windows of the camper.

"What about—about like, dogs and stuff?" William said. "Deer? What do you do with them?"

"Not endangered," the cop said, taking advantage of the break in traffic to step back around the bear, towards his car. "Some people eat the shit, I've heard, I don't know." He hooked the brim of his stiff hat to his car. "We've got shovels, y'know. If it's impeding traffic, we help it into the ditch."

William nodded.

"Him?" he said, about the bear.

The cop looked down to it too.

"Was it in your way as a motorist, Mr.. . . ?"

William looked away.

"Pinzer," he said, like he'd been saying it his whole life. Then he shook his head no, it hadn't been in his way.

The cop flashed his light down onto the truck again.

"You've got four wheel drive on her?"

William nodded.

The cop shrugged. "This is Louisiana," he said. "I mean, I'd never advise leaving the blacktop unless I had to, know?"

"I'm careful," William said.

The cop nodded, spit.

"Where to?"

"My sister. Shreveport."

The cop touched something off the right lens of the glasses he had hooked in his pocket.

"Fucking *bear*," he said.

"I know," William said back, and they smiled together.

Two minutes later, the cop was gone.

William looked at the bear for maybe thirty seconds more, thanking it, then pushed it as far into the road as he could. He hadn't lied to the cop, though: he didn't want it. A bear would draw too much attention.

The first truck that hit it caught it across its hindquarters, forcing all the air and gases in its body up past its throat, past its voice box.

William screamed with it.

Three miles after the next rest stop—Louisiana, still—next to a burned-out trailer house with trees growing all around it, William hung his bubble-gum pink ice cream cone from the rearview, turned the cargo light on.

Lobo was there, and the Shepherd mix he was supposed to call Max and feed canned food twice a day, and the Golden Retriever with the red handkerchief tied around his neck like a cartoon dog.

They were dead, of course, lined up against the naked body of the woman as if nursing.

Her name was *M*-something, William didn't know.

She had been an accident. Not on purpose. From Birmingham.

William stepped up into the camper with her and laid sideways behind her, stroking the top of her arm, getting hard again.

But there was no time for that.

William closed his eyes, told himself that, that there was no time, then let his hand fall to the soft muzzle of one of the dogs, and came anyway five minutes later, his hand against the dog's dry tongue, the place where the girl's nipple had been, then he cried into her matted hair, apologized. Hit the side of his hand again and again into the bed of the truck, until that hand was numb. And then the rest of him too. Just cold, nothing.

He was ready.

Twenty miles deeper into Louisiana, at a truck stop, he pulled over, walked back to his passenger side rear tire, and popped the camper shell open.

In the dead space between trucks pulling out of second gear, building speed for the interstate, he slung Lobo out into the ribbon of shiny asphalt, where the tires ran. He weighed half again as much as he had, was pregnant with the girl now. Pieces of her anyway.

In the back of the truck, on the tarp, William had laid out her arms, all four pieces of her legs, and the four quarters of her torso. From biggest to smallest. The head he ran over with his truck again and again, until there was nothing left of the teeth or any of it, and then he buried it, peed a circle around it to keep guard.

Then it was back to the tarp.

Working in the dim glow of the cargo lamp, he opened the three dogs from sternum to asshole, cleaned them out, and tried to fit what he could into each: an arm, part of a ribcage, a lower leg. When he was done, the dogs sewn up with pig string, William had nodded, stood from his work, and caught the shadow of something in the door of the burned-out trailer behind him.

He turned the cargo light off—everything calm, no problem—folded the tarp up, pushed the dogs carefully back under the camper, then stood facing the trailer for twelve minutes.

Nothing moved. He dared it to, but nothing did.

Finally he nodded, narrowed his eyes, and marked the place in his mind, so he could come back sometime when he could leave what was in his truck in his truck.

Not tonight, though.

Four miles back, he'd already been seeing the signs for the truck stop, could feel a flat coming on.

He didn't even have to get the jack out this time. Just opened the tailgate, positioned Lobo on the road, then closed the tailgate, pulled away. At first, years ago, he'd always had to wait, to see the trucks come, watch them flatten all the bones at once, human and canine, but now, now he knew it happened whether he was there or not. The only other choice would be someone stopping to autopsy this dog that had already been hit. Or to move it out of the way. But only the state cops did that, and this was a county road, or parish, whatever things were in Louisiana.

The next dog he left on an exit ramp, in the intersection, where everybody was supposed to yield.

The Golden Retriever with the red handkerchief he simply stood up with a dry branch in a low spot on the service road, eighteen miles down from Lobo. Stood him up, circled back, then ran him down, leaning into his horn at the last minute, closing his eyes to the thumping from underneath, the crunching—*Marissa*, that had been it—then downshifting for the hill ahead, for Beaumont.

2.

Four months later—Houston—William tried for the third time to balance his empty beer can on the four-wheel-drive shifter of the Chevy he had now. For a moment, maybe, it held, staying there for him, but then fell into the passenger side floorboard with the rest.

He was sitting in the first visitor row of the downtown hospital.

The Chevy was because that state cop had caressed the Ford with his flashlight. William had tried to forget it, tried not to feel the heat the flashlight had pulled across the skin of his truck, the sharp-edged shadows the trim and fender flares had cast, but it was too much. Each time since then that he'd walked up on the truck from that angle—after work (stacking transmissions), after the bar, after buying all the newspapers he was in—it had been the same: that night, the bear. And because it was like that for him, it had to be for the cop, too. So the Ford had to go.

William had sold it to one of the mechanics at his work, Al, who never looked anybody in the eye but had told William once that he'd started out at the shop scraping gaskets too. That if William just stuck around long enough, a sentence he finished by studying the insulation chicken-wired to the metal walls.

William had shrugged, looked out at the traffic, Al peeling up a line of the seal that had been under the camper shell. Then, William had been saving it, the shell, for his next Ford, but that was what he'd sold the *first* Ford for, right?

Now it was in his efficiency apartment, the camper, leaned up over the window.

He didn't know what to do with it.

The Chevy was one the garage across the street had applied for the title for, in lieu of payment for services. The title had come back salvage; the manager let William have it for eight hundred. Alone in the parking lot after hours, William sifted through the cab, the gum wrappers, beer caps, and dimes that had settled behind the seat. The stack of magazines by the seat adjustment: *Shaved, Bare, Lassie.*

William dropped them into the asphalt, backing away, shaking his head no, he wasn't like that anymore.

But then the magazines started opening by themselves, in the wind.

After three weeks, William made himself throw them away in fourteen separate dumpsters. It was too late, though; his beard was thick again, full. He replaced the magazines under the seat with clippings of himself: a missing girl in Pensacola, another just outside Hattiesburg. Sixteen over the last nine and a half years, the first two still buried in plastic dropcloths, soaked first in ammonia, then pesticide, then gear oil. So none of the gas of decay would work its way up through the soil.

He'd put them side by side, east and west, face-up.

The first time he'd gone back to see them, grass was growing everywhere but the two rectangles where they were.

William had started breathing hard, too hard, and returned with fertilizer, Bermuda grass seeds, finally flowers. They all died, until he understood: the ground was dead, it needed life.

William had nodded, unzipped his pants, and, over the course of five weeks, left enough of his seed on the graves that the soil took on a richer color, and then a plant of some sort raised its head. William named it Baby Green, thought about it when he wasn't there, then watched it stand up straight, establishing itself.

Once, William reached down to touch it, just once, but then saw something watching him across the field.

It was a dog, her teats heavy, dragging.

William stood and she didn't move, didn't move. Like she knew.

Four weeks after that, going back to check on Baby Green, sure that a raccoon was digging the girls up for their silver rings, William's headlights caught eleven perfect little puppies walking across the road. Their shadows were taller than his headlights could reach.

William opened his door, stepped down, and the mother dog came for him from the tall grass, and it was all slow motion, overfull with meaning, with detail.

At the last moment he pushed her aside with his boot, stepped back into the truck. Rolled forward carefully, respectfully.

After that, he started noticing all the dead animals along the interstate.

Baby Green was still out there too, William knew. A fairy tale beanstalk he could never see again, because the graves were probably staked out by patient men with mirrored sunglasses.

In the parking lot of the hospital, William opened a fifth beer. Some of it splashed onto the leg of his jeans and he stood up. It made it to the seat of his pants anyway. The crack of his ass.

She would never talk to him now.

Her name was Julia. A caramel-colored nurse.

William had got her name off her nameplate by timing his entrance with her exit a week ago, then done it again, in case she'd just been borrowing somebody's ID that night.

Julia.

She got off every night at eleven. Wore a series of headbands, probably to keep her hair out of patients' faces. Or to keep them from falling in love with her.

Tonight, William watched the waist of her aquamarine scrubs for a zip key, a handheld radio. The best forty-five seconds of the night were her, stepping across the crosswalk, dipping her head down for the cell phone, the call she only made once she was outside the magnets and radiation of the hospital.

There was never any blood on her scrubs, never anybody walking with her. Just Julia, Julia.

William smiled, nodded, and turned his truck on just after she'd passed, so his brake lights could turn her red in his side mirror.

She never looked back.

William drank the fifth beer down, eased out of Visitor Parking, past the security booth which pulled the blinds down at five-thirty, and out into the road. For a moment at thirty-five miles per hour, there was a squirrel in the road, flattened to the pavement.

William said it aloud: "Squirrels."

They didn't hold anything.

What he needed now, and what he knew he didn't need, was a camper shell for the Chevy. The one in his apartment he had pieced up with a hacksaw and a pair of tin snips, then finally just carried the last four big pieces away in the bed of his truck, left them in four different alleys, upside down to catch rain, become a nuisance, a mosquito pool, the edges sharp enough that only the garbage men with their thick, city-bought gloves would be able to lift them. And garbage men didn't care about anything. William knew; it was one of the jobs his father had taken, after the Army, before all the wine coolers that didn't count as drinking, that didn't break any promises.

Again William remembered building forts with his brother in the living room.

Their father was always the Indian. The one who had taken their mother away.

William slammed his fist into the horn of the Chevy. It honked. The man in the leather vest behind the counter of the pawnshop ratcheted his head around to the sound, then up the hood to William.

William looked away, pursed his lips. Backed out.

The paper had said they had camper shells, but it was just to get the hunters in, sell them a gun. William didn't need a *gun*, though. He used his blinker to get in front of a blue El Camino. What he needed was a *camper* shell. Because if he didn't get one, he would be back to tarps, and wouldn't be able to drive on the interstate anymore, because the truckers would see, radio ahead.

Because because because.

William had three hundred dollars in his pocket, part of it an advance on his paycheck, part left over from selling the Ford.

That was another reason he was leaving Houston: every day, he had to see his old truck across the road, cocked at an angle against the chain link, by the parts cars.

Finally, in the classifieds, William found a camper shell. It was supposed to be north of town, and east. Tomball, in the crotch of I-10 and I-45. He had to call twice for directions, then listen for real the second time. Each time, the man who answered the phone thought William was calling about a help wanted ad, somebody to replace his son. One hour later—eight miles—William turned up the long driveway of the farm house, slowed alongside the camper shell. It was on an old Gentleman Jim, had been painted black and gold to match the truck, then had the paint baked on.

William stepped out, ran his hand over the warm fiberglass then looked at his palm. It was glittering. Past it, the old man, picking his way through all the other junked cars. He held his hand out, looked over William's shoulder at his Chevy. It was gold and white, the colors of some oil company from West Texas.

The old man nodded.

"It matches," he said. "The gold, right?"

The old man was sixty-eight, maybe seventy-four. A house twice as old as him, at the end of a series of dirt roads that were better than any fence. Most of the land around the house was weeds, some of it on the downslope spongy with swampwater, thick with frogs.

William looked to the Gentleman Jim then raised one cheek, narrowing that eye. He shook his head no.

"You don't think it'll fit," the old man said. "It will."

"I know," William said. "But—the paint, I mean. You can't just spray fiberglass yourself."

The old man agreed.

"Seventy then," he said, no eye contact.

William shrugged, looked to the shell again. The ad in the paper had an *OBO* after the *$100*. "I don't know," he said. Overhead, one small airplane whined just as another—yellow—broke from the line of trees down the hill from the man's house.

William flinched backwards, stumbled into the grass.

The old man looked to the plane to let William avoid the embarrassment of trying to stand as if nothing had happened.

"Maniacs," he said. "There should be a law."

It was a cropduster. The racks of nozzles, the bitter smell in the air, then, just all at once, no smell at all. William knew the herbicide had numbed his nose. He still couldn't talk.

"Fifty," the old man said, toeing the ground.

William opened the envelope from his shirt pocket, counted out the three bills, and then the old man insisted on a receipt, was gone for ten minutes to the house, for pen and paper.

William ducked again the next time the plane came, but this time saw a roll of toilet paper trail down from it. It was how the pilots flew when they didn't have a spotter—how they marked their passes.

"Maniac," William said to the plane, low, smiling, then got the wrenches and pliers and flat-head from his truck, started getting the camper ready to move off the Gentleman Jim.

When the old man came back with his receipt the SOLD TO part was blank. William wrote in *Bill Dozier* then laid on his back in the bed of the Gentleman Jim, placed the soles of his boots against the underside of the camper shell. At first, pushing with his legs, it just rained fiberglass down onto him—spun light—but then the foam seal on one side gave, then the other, and the camper shell shifted towards the rear of the truck. The old man stepped forward to take its weight, and, behind him, looking between his legs, there was a large, dark dog, loping through the grass.

The old man followed William's eyes, turned, then called something out to the dog, a name William didn't quite catch. *Blanco? Blackie?*

"He didn't hear you," William said.

The old man laughed without smiling. "He heard me," he said.

Moments later, the black dog was there. A puppy in an adult dog body, unable to stand still. Excited just to be alive for another perfect day.

William let himself pet it between the shoulder blades. The dog craned its head around, to lick the sweat from William's wrist.

William looked up, for the plane he was hearing again. It was what the dog had been chasing, probably. The shadow coursing along the ground, blackening a tree for a moment, so that it looked new again when the plane was gone.

William understood.

He stepped down from the tailgate of the Gentleman Jim, all his weight on his left arm for a breath, the shoulder there forever torn.

"What?" the old man asked.

William realized he was making a noise in his throat.

"Nothing," he said, then took the old man's eyes away from that side of his body, ran his other hand along the side window of the camper, in appreciation. All that was left now was to back his truck up, work the camper from one to the other, and screw it down. The foam kit, he would get in town. Then he could back the truck into the empty bay at work, chock the shell up on blocks, sand down the bed rails.

But that was all later. Everything was later, nothing was now. Just the sound of that cropduster, the black dog streaking across the field.

William was sure the plane wasn't going to clear the trees this time.

He opened his mouth to tell the dog, but the old man was still watching him, following his arm out to the dog, an acre away already.

"Need one?" he said.

It was a joke.

Across the field, the yellow plane crashed up into the sky again, tearing away from the earth.

"Not yet," William said, swallowing his smile.

Not yet.

Three six-packs later, William sat up against the sink of his apartment and cried and cried. Like a baby, like a goddamn girl.

The one name he never gave anybody was William H. Bonney. Billy the Kid.

Surrounded by couch cushions in the living room, he had been Billy the Kid, his brother Jesse James, because his name had started with a *J*.

Their father's Indian name was Bites All the Way Through, was Kicks Open the Door Until the House Falls Over, was Born With Teeth, was Custer. This was when they didn't understand, thought Custer was Indian.

William rubbed heat into his shoulder and drank another beer, promised Julia that it was going to be all right this time. That he didn't have to do anything. And then he said it out loud, like a defense, like the only logical answer—*cowboys and Indians, Dad*—but heard again his shoulder tearing, like the sound had never even left his body after all these years, had just been traveling back and forth along the guitar-string tendons of his neck, burrowing into his inner ear.

The reason his dad had been jerking him up from the couch was because they weren't supposed to play on the couch like that anymore. Because their mom was going to be home soon.

William reeled his pocket watch up, studied it.

Julia was in the eighth hour of her shift, probably. Holding the pad of her middle finger to a patient's pulse, counting under her breath. The clock ticking, moving, each second two cents to her maybe, or more—a nickel? William had no idea how much a nurse made.

He said it again, cowboys and Indians, then put himself back into the pound. As Pinzer. Walking down the hall behind the caramel-colored attendant who's already off the clock. The pound where she has her keys zipped out from her belt, is twirling them around her index finger, letting them swing back to her palm again and again.

William follows, follows, all the dogs in their runs barking and barking, but no sound.

"This one," he says, about a Husky, then, about a chocolate Lab with child eyes, "No, this one."

The attendant in front of him smiles, keeps swishing back and forth, *knows*, and William follows her around one corner, then another, and then she's waiting for him with a hose. It's on, just trickling because she knows how to work it. She asks if he's thirsty and he says yes, drinks. When he looks up, she's unlocking an empty run.

He walks in behind her because she wants him too. She's already stepping out of her scrubs, using her feet to pull the loose pants down each leg.

William smiles at the tan lines he wouldn't have expected on her, how close the top line of her bikini dips to her nipple, how close her aureole is to the sun—how wide it is, spreading like a stain, like she was dipped in something then laid out on her back—then sees that his hand is in his pants, like he told himself to do in the parking lot, and then she comes to him, hooking one brown leg around his side, grinding her warmth up against him, breathing into his ear, and that was the way he came back to his kitchen: hard, all the air in his apartment compressed in his lungs. Pushing with his heels on the linoleum.

He barely made it to the hospital in time, then came just as Julia stepped into the crosswalk, gushing onto his chest and stomach so much he thought that maybe he was bleeding somehow, that he was shooting spinal fluid, then gagging from the thought of it, splashing hot vomit into the tilted well of the speedometer, down along the steering column to the fire-wall. Crying still, because he knew from the way he'd taken the caramel-colored pound attendant, from the way he'd been *about* to take her, the way she turned around for him, resting the tips of her fingers on the stained concrete, he knew she was pregnant now with a litter of puppies that were going to eat her the first chance they got.

Two days later Al called him from the shop, to ask where he wanted his check mailed. What there was of it, after the advance.

"I'll come get it," William said.

"Not a good idea, hoss," Al said back, low enough that William knew Mitch was standing in the bay by the phone.

"Sorry," William said, when it seemed like Al was waiting for him to say something.

"Where you been?"

"My shoulder," William lied.

Al laughed—shaped his breath into a laugh, it sounded like. So he wouldn't have to smile.

"This a workman's comp issue?" he said, quieter, the punchline.

William shrugged.

After that, Al said something, William said something— none of it mattered, was like other people talking—and then William put the phone back on its cradle.

He hadn't been back to the hospital since the night he'd thrown up all his love for Julia, then fingered it back in. Off his chest too, the strings matting his beard. Since the night he'd started his truck when it was already running, the metal-on-bone sound of his flywheel jerking her head around in his side mirror, her hair in the brake lights sideways from her body for one perfect instant—a communion. A moment they'd shared, the rabbit recognizing a blind spot in the trail it had been walking for weeks now.

An accident.

William leaned into the wall by the phone and apologized to her again. Because now he had no choice—she knew his truck, had marked how the black and gold camper shell didn't fit the oil-field pale body. Because now she was trying to remember if it had been there the night before, or was it last week? She was probably making up a history for him, even, William: that his brother was in ICU, that he was driving up from Galveston each night just to sit by the hospital bed, struggle through the day's paper out loud.

Like that could have saved James. Like anything could have.

In his apartment, William smiled.

Now that he had to do it, it would be easy.

He spent the rest of the afternoon wiping down his apartment, even the underside of the toilet lid, the inside of the P-trap in the kitchen, then an hour trying to fit the magnet from the mouthpiece of the phone up into the earpiece, then two minutes locking the door behind him, then dusk at a filling station, for the Chevy's two tanks, then lining the camper shell with black RTV sealant, because he hadn't had time for the foam kit. All that was left was answering an index card that had been posted at the animal clinic with a red tack in the shape of a heart. An index card that had been posted just for him.

The woman who answered the door was a girl. Eleven, twelve. Her eyes tracked all the way up William. His hands were already in his pocket, his sunglasses hooked into his flannel shirt.

"Hello," he said.

The girl called behind her, for her mother.

She was even better. William looked down along the porch, steadied himself on the wall.

"Yes?" the mother said, one hand on her daughter's shoulder, ready to pull the girl into the house, step between.

William felt his eyes heat up about this.

"The—the Lhasa," he said, like a question.

The mother tried looking past him, for his truck, but it was down the street where some Mexicans were working a lawn.

"You're. . . ?" the mother started.

William opened his mouth, stepped back in apology.

"Just—sorry, sorry. I just . . . my daughter, I'm seeing her this weekend."

The mother looked up to him, to his eyes.

"Her birthday," he explained, and then it was there, the Lhasa, yapping, its tiny forepaws edging past the weather-stripping on the floor.

The mother nodded. A cordless phone in her hand. William wondered how anybody ever strangled anybody anymore.

The index card had said FREE TO GOOD HOME.

The mother nodded down to William's left hand. His naked ring finger.

In return, he shrugged, squinted away, down the street, to the sound of a weed-eater or an edger.

"She looks like her," he said finally, lifting his chin to the daughter.

The daughter shrank to her mother's leg some.

Inside, William smiled. Outside, he shrugged again, shook his head no. Arranged his face into an outside smile too.

"I'm lying," he said, like it had been going to come out anyway. "She's—Kimbo. She's not mine. My brother's girl. Niece. I just like to . . . y'know. Pretend."

"Maybe your brother can—" the mother started, but William closed his eyes tight, shook his head no.

"He can't," he said.

That part wasn't a lie.

Two minutes later, the mother calling her husband, 'to let him know about Vanessa,' the dog—really just an excuse to leave the phone on, to let William *know* the phone was on— William stepped into the house, felt like he was balancing on the welcome mat. He looked back, where he'd just been, on the porch: there was no one watching.

Two fer Tuesday, he said to himself, a thing he'd been hearing on the radio, and stepped off, onto the pale, absorbent carpet of the living room.

This time he parked in the second row of Visitor's, first the other way, nosed away from the hospital, so she would just be seeing the top of the camper, the tailgate, but then realizing in a desperate rush that that's what she'd already seen when he'd started his already-started truck last week. He backed out, turned around and reversed into the slot, scratching the tires with each gear change, then didn't let himself drink any beer except one, and then another to hide the first, to stop his hands from shaking, and finally just three, to get it over with.

From the floorboard with all the cans, Vanessa stared at him.

He smiled down to her, patted her on the head.

Her bowl and extra collar and her favorite pink ball were in three dumpsters on three different streets. The mother and daughter had insisted William take them. The only thing he'd kept was the rhinestone leash, but then, walking away from their house, he hadn't even used it. Instead, he'd carried Vanessa like a baby, like they wanted him to, whispering down into her left ear that he knew what she tasted like, yes he did yes he did.

Everything was falling into place. Like always.

10:30 came and went, then 10:32, then 10:35. Two hours later, it was almost 11:00. William stroked his beard down along his jaw, blinked too much, and rocked in his seat, went through the checklist again, making sure.

When she walked out all at once, looking into her purse, he straightened his right leg hard, washing the cars in his side mirrors angry red, look-at-me-I'm-the-I-10-killer-give-away red, but then knew it was now, it was now. Because once she got her cell phone open—

It was the only reason he wasn't simply parked by her car, out in B.

Now, *now*.

He stepped from his truck, pulled Vanessa down to the end of his row, opposite the truck. Knew the rhinestones were going to give him away, that he should just—

But no: *now*.

This.

It was why they were alone here in the middle of the city, charmed, nobody walking in from the parking lot, nobody pushing through the exit doors.

William smiled, nodded.

She was four long steps from the crosswalk now, the phone in her hand, her finger to the call button, she was four, three steps from the crosswalk when William chocked up on the leash with his right hand, still holding the loop in his left. Like that, he could lift Vanessa, swing her, her collar already tightened then double-checked.

One time around, then two, the soft Lhasa body stiff at the end of the leash, then more slack, like a hammer throw, then he let her go into the sky, followed through with his right arm.

Five seconds, then Vanessa fell into the crosswalk Julia should have been using, for safety.

Julia stopped, the cell to her ear, ringing probably, and she looked at it, the dog, then looked up into the sky, lowered the phone.

There were maybe one thousand things that could happen now.

William knew she would accept any of them, too: a man in an almost-white truck with a black camper, pulling out of the Visitor's lot, stopping at the small, white, twitching dog, stepping out, locking eyes with Julia, asking her without words what happened, his truck too loud so she has to take a step closer, another step, and by then she's already started dying.

From a phone booth at a gas station at the Texas state line, William called to confess, to tell her everything, the caramel-colored pound attendant, that he loves her, that he was confused, that he's sorry, that she doesn't *understand*, but then he didn't know her name. So he explained her to the pound's night attendant, explained her too well—her nipples under her scrub shirt, how she was one of those girls who wore a tank top instead of a bra—then asked about the pregnant dog. If her puppies were running around the waiting room already, pulling all the stuffing from all the chairs. If their eyes were open yet or if they were still blind.

The attendant on the other end laughed through his nose.

"Blind," he said, "yeah. Technically, I mean. If you count dead."

William leaned deeper into the phone booth.

"And the—the mother?"

The attendant laughed again, said William wasn't shitting about Charla, there, the house *pointer*, then laughed some more, hung up while he was doing it so that William had to picture him sitting there, alone in the pound, eyes teared up from laughing. At William.

He turned to his truck, knew suddenly in the way he knew things that he was parked too close to the trash can. That the clerk or the clerk's manager or a homeless person or a monkey escaped from the circus was going to reach into the trash, pull out the three strips William had just cut the junk license plates into.

William shook his head no, wiped the phone down, then almost ran across the concrete to the truck, to the trashcan, pushing his arm as deep as he could into it, deep enough that he had to turn his head away, point his chin up. The clerk standing at the glass door, watching.

William raised his other hand, waved, made himself smile as if this were all some big mistake—the credit card itself, instead of the receipt, the beer bottle instead of the cap.

The clerk raised his hand back hesitantly, his face wrenched into a fake smile as well.

William left with two of the license plate strips, a cut finger wrapped in electric tape, and Julia, asleep in back, tied and gagged under the tarp, the tarp held down with toolboxes with real tools in them (Mitch's), and a cooler with bumper stickers all over it, beer inside.

She wasn't awake yet.

William apologized to her again, for how cold the tarp was going to be for her, naked like that. The tips of her breasts stiff against the black, woven plastic.

Drive, he told himself. Miles, miles, go go go.

Louisiana was a familiar bog of smells and alligator eyes.

William held the wheel with both hands, accidentally looked up to a cab-over passing him slow in the left lane, and knew for an instant it was his father, straightened his back into the seat for the coolness of the wine cooler bottle, whooshing by.

When it never came, the truck driver just nodded, pulled ahead in a way that William knew he had read the last number called on Julia's cell phone. It was open on the seat beside him, its small screen glowing green, a beacon.

William made himself slow down to sixty, spit the taste of adrenaline out the window. He turned the radio up.

The last person he'd seen in Texas, the last person who could identify him, had been a paramedic pushing an empty gurney across the Emergency lane, from one red curb to another. William had stopped, and the paramedic had raised his fingers on the aluminum tubing, in thanks.

"No problem," William said, both in the Emergency lane and in Louisiana, then nodded back instead of waving, because her hair had still been in his fingers, from pulling her into the cab, slamming her face into the dashboard three times fast.

All she had left behind was one shoe, but he'd backed up, leaned down for it, then pulled away, no headlights.

Three miles past a rest stop—always three miles, because by then the truckers would be into their tall gears, be making too much time to stop—three miles past a rest stop, he finally climbed back through the sliding rear window he'd fed her through in Houston.

The radio was still on, the old, nasal country William hated drifting in from the cab.

But Julia.

He lay down beside her, the tarp still between them. Used his finger to find her mouth then pushed the very tip of his knife through the tarp and through the duct tape stretched across her lower face.

She was awake. Just a small hole in a piece of black plastic.

William said her name and she didn't say anything back.

The tape across her lower face was parallel to the tape across her forehead, keeping the back of her head to the bed of the truck. William had pushed her bangs out of the way as much as he could.

He came on her stomach and she never felt it.

Julia.

If he did everything right this time, she might last four days, maybe even five. Six was the record but he knew better than to go longer, that they would get a power over him then.

"You're a nurse," he told her, instead of everything else.

She moved. It was maybe a nod.

William nodded with her, cut a hole over her left eye but messed up, had to do the right instead.

He held the green display of the cell phone up to the hole, at all the distances between two inches and a foot.

"Who's Robert?" he asked, using the same voice he'd used to tell her she was a nurse.

Robert was from her message log. Robert Mendes.

Julia moved again but this time it was no, a plea with the length of her body.

William smiled, laid back beside her, staring at the roof of the camper shell, and told her to look at all the fiberglass threads, how they made a cocoon, how that meant that the two of them were moths, about to lift up into the hot air over I-10, and then he put the mask he'd bought at the store over the shape of her face, straddled her hips, cut a hole over the tip of one breast, and fed.

Two days later William took her down to see the water, the ocean. Because sunsets on the Gulf are romantic.

He carried her from the bed of the truck to the busted sand, to the line of darkness that meant it was wet, and even took the new tape off her mouth. There was no one for miles. He watched her watch the light on the water. She was shivering. There was nothing he could do for the fever. Once he'd tried, feeding a girl named Roberta aspirin at regular intervals, but it thinned her blood so much that she bled out on the second day, and then kept bleeding, long after her heart wasn't even pushing the blood anymore.

But Julia.

William smiled. His knees were up on either side of her, his arms around them, hands clasped between his knees.

They were still in Louisiana. William had decided that the first night: that she was going to be a Louisiana girl. That she would be more comfortable there—the humidity, the green. It would be like Houston for her. They weren't calling him anything there yet. Last year in Florida, in one paper he'd been the I-10 Killer, and in another, on the same day, he was Ponce de Leon. He'd looked it up in a public library in Jacksonville that afternoon: Ponce de Leon, traveling along what would become the interstate, looking for the fountain of youth.

For four days at a time anyway. Six if the girl was strong enough.

In the dying sun, William saw that Julia's wounds were healing. Something about the melanin of dark girls, probably. Her foot was in the sand, though. Deeper than the sun could reach. And she wasn't going anywhere with that foot. The one time she tried, slumping sideways away from him, he had to hit her with the back of his hand, was already catching her fast enough that the tips of her hair just left ghost lines in the sand.

So she wouldn't choke, he cradled her head in his lap, stroked her hair away from her face, along his leg, the weight of it on his thigh no more than a shadow.

It wasn't too late to take her to a hospital. Or to call 911 from a payphone, leave her there. Or sit her down at the bus stop, her silver little phone blinking *Robert Mendes*.

William closed his eyes, swallowed. In her breast closest to him there was a hole. It was leaking. Not blood, but something thicker, more clear. William smeared it around the edge of the hole, then, half on accident, slipped his finger in to the second knuckle, saw his brother James for a flash and clamped his eyes shut against that, curled his finger deep enough in Julia's breast that she straightened out, standing on her heels and the back of her head.

William opened his mouth to tell her to stop this, to keep James and his chickenwire chest out of this sunset, that she didn't even *know* about it, or about their dad poking his finger into it too hard, and the way her head nodded forward on her neck, he knew she understood. She was telling him it was all right, that it had always been all right.

Breathing too hard, his eyes wet, William forced another finger into that hole, and then his hand, the skin stretching to swallow him, and then he flexed his fingers inside the warm wet insides of her breast so that his knuckles were like little dome-headed puppies waking up in there, their eyes not even open yet.

William's other hand dealt with himself, urgently.

They were the only two people in the world.

When it was over and done with, he arranged Julia's hair all in a line, like it had been combed. Her head eased over into his lap again, some muscle in her neck drawing tight. And William wasn't crying. He thinned his lips so anybody could see that he wasn't crying.

He looked out to the water again, his fingers still in Julia's hair.

"You like dogs?" he asked her, and when her head moved again, that one stubborn muscle giving up, he smiled, told her good, that was good. Maybe he would have to get her a dog, then. A big one.

45

3.

The mask he made her wear when she was under the tarp was Little Bo Peep, only he'd pulled the hair away from it, so it was just those baby-fat cheeks, the red Shirley Temple lips he kept having to lipstick over. It was hard, though, getting the lipstick straight, not smearing it on the porcelain skin, and no matter how long he let it dry, it still made his mouth look like he'd just eaten a cherry lollipop.

Julia was in her third day.

After he'd told her about James on accident, and after she'd figured out that she was in a Gentleman *Jim* camper, he'd had to reach in through the tear duct of her bad eye with a coat hanger, pull everything he'd told her out, swallow it back down.

She was a doll, now.

Then it was her fourth day. The cab of the truck was rolling with Weimaraner-Pit puppies. They had been in a box by a vegetable stand. William had paid eight dollars for each of them, eighty-eight dollars in all. This was before the coat hanger, when he was sure Julia was going to live months and months, and happily ever after. When it made sense to buy the dogs young, wait for them to grow.

Now he was going to have to get an extra dog just to hide

them in. Like the unborn. Maybe he could even sew their eyes shut again, or superglue them, or—

William shook his head no. That he was never going to do this again. That it was *wrong*. That Julia didn't count because she was an accident, a victim of his weakness.

But then he remembered James and his friends, catching farm dogs and starving them down for three or four days, then putting them in the cotton trailer with a fat little cottontail. Watching that cottontail run around and around the trailer and finally climb the wire fence, making the kind of sounds a rabbit only ever makes once.

It was too complicated for Julia to ever understand. For any of them to.

Going back to the rabbit days after, after the dog had caught her and didn't know what to do with her. Going back to her and the boy that was standing there, watching through the fence. Maggots roiling out of the carcass, the boy smiling, saying they were babies, that she was having babies, that he was going to catch one, keep it.

William nodded, veered off the road, corrected the right amount.

The rabbit babies. It was funny. Maggots, worms, like the blind white things wriggling in the puppies' shit now.

William kept the windows up to punish himself, teach himself a lesson. Tried to drink a beer but gagged on it, spit up onto his chest. Called out to Julia through the sliding glass, no answer.

The sign on the side of the road said to yield.

William backed up to it, threw beer cans at it until his floor-board was empty.

Above him, the clouds were musty, motionless. His head-lights giving him a shadow with a head shaped like the yield sign, like he was an alien.

He turned them off, backed into the trees, and tried to get the smallest of the puppies to feed from a slit in the plastic he cut over Julia's good breast, then held its mouth there until his arm was trembling. Until his whole body was.

Beside her still was the coat hanger, black from the lighter he'd held all along it, to clean it. Because she was a nurse: hygiene would be important to her.

William nestled into the plastic alongside her, kept his eyes open until the fifth day.

At a gas station, the truck parked by the propane tanks, locked and double-locked, William shaved earlier than he ever had before, saw himself in the mirror so clean. A different person. A new one.

He cupped his chin in his hand, tilting his head left then right.

On the door by the clerk—already—was a black and white photocopy of Julia. Julia Mendes.

William pretended it wasn't there.

For six hours now he had been thinking about the boy and the rabbit, the boy saying how he was going to keep one.

William kept saying it to himself like that, trying it on: *I'm going to keep one.*

Not Julia, it was too late for her. But the Weimaraner-Pit puppies. One of them. A boy one. He would ride shotgun with William, guard the truck for him when he couldn't be with it.

William didn't know how he hadn't thought of it years before.

He walked the two aisles of the store for canned dog food, or beef stew, but it was just oil and paper plates and chips.

"Where is it?" he asked the clerk.

"What?"

"Dog stuff."

The clerk smiled, shook his head no.

"For a puppy, I mean," William said, tapping himself on the side of the head to remember better. "Puppy food."

The man studied William now.

"Like milk, you mean?" he said.

William brought the largest puppy in to show. The clerk took it over the counter, holding it expertly, in a way that made William immediately know he was going to trust this clerk forever.

The clerk turned his attention to the pup, held it up to his face and put his nose to the sharp little mouth.

"Sweet," he said. "Weaning?"

William forgot to blink for too long, made himself, then suddenly couldn't stop, just shook his head no. "She doesn't have any—she's dry, I mean," he said.

The clerk shrugged.

"Milk, then," he said, handing the puppy back. "Who knows, right?"

William paid for two gallons, left, but the puppy wouldn't drink any of it, even when he pulled over, leaked it into the cup of flesh that had been Julia's nipple. Even when he leaked it onto his own.

He shook his head no, no, then just drove faster than he knew he should have, fast enough to get caught and *deserve* to get caught, but no blue lights flashed, everyone knew he was charmed, probably even wanted him doing what he did.

But the puppies.

He smiled, told them it was going to be all right, then, taking a road around some nothing-town, found himself easing through a ditch where a livestock trailer had overturned days ago. The cows were still there. William nodded, didn't have to look to either side to see his father, moving among them right after the wreck, his sickle glinting moonlight.

Just past the cows were the dogs that had come to the smell. Green eyes in the tall grass, one of them moving to chase the truck, then all of them moving.

William nodded like this was the way it was supposed to be.

A quarter mile down, after the most long-winded of the dogs had fallen away, William saw what had to be there: one of the dogs, already run over.

He watched it in his headlights until he was sure it wasn't going to rise, then stepped down, inspected. It was huge, a Rott like Lobo maybe, but bigger, with some Shepherd or something in it. Big like the bear cub.

William cradled its stiff body to his chest, peeled it from the asphalt, and put it on Julia's feet, to keep her warm.

It was tonight. The dog had been a sign.

Three hours later, dawn not even a smell yet, William had two more dogs in the camper shell. Both Spaniel size. The third he had to go into town for, run down the address. It was a Lab, though, would hold enough to be worth the trouble.

Now all he needed was a place to work.

He stepped back up onto the interstate, knew immediately where he was, where the rest stops were each way, and it was comfortable, right. He kept the Chevy at sixty-five, let the big trucks slam past him for Florida, and blinked his lights, letting them pull back into his lane.

It was during one such black moment—headlights off—that the lightbar flared up behind him.

He touched his brakes, pulled his lights back on, and coasted to the side.

The cop followed his flashlight along the side of the truck, stood at an angle to the window William had already rolled down. The light played across both of William's hands, gripped onto the wheel in plain sight. The back of them was white, dusted with the same hair his forearm was. The palms were black with blood, from the Lab.

"Sir," the cop said.

"Officer?" William said back, turning his eyes from the light.

It was the same cop from the bear. The cop who knew the Ford. It was his county, his stretch of the interstate.

"I do something. . . ?" William led off.

The officer had his beam of light shining pale through the tinted side window of the camper. And then he got the smell from the cab, stepped back, his hand falling to the butt of his gun.

"What the hell—?" he said.

William shrugged.

"Dogs," he said, and pushed back into the bench seat, giving the officer a better angle on the puppies in the floorboard. The cardboard barrier William had cut, to keep them from the pedals.

The cop was breathing hard now, trying to.

"Where—where?"

"Weimaraners," William said, a half lie. "Delivering them for my sister."

"Your sister?"

William hooked his chin up the road.

"Not crossing any state lines," he said. "Don't worry."

The cop blinked, wiped his eyes with the back of his sleeve, and tapped his flashlight against the camper.

William kept his hands on the wheel, looked through the sliding glass behind him.

The other dogs were back there. They were moving, undulating, as if asleep: Julia, kicking slow under the tarp "Those ones are mine," William said.

"All of them?"

Through the tinted side glass, the blood on the two smaller dogs' coats would be the liver stains of a Springer Spaniel. And the bigger two dogs were black.

William nodded.

"Shouldn't they be—awake?" the cop said, tapping the glass again.

William smiled, caught.

"Benadryl," he said. "I should give them Dramamine, I know, but shit. You know what that costs?"

"Allergy medicine?"

William nodded, almost snapped, pictured the blood from the Lab spattering from his fingers to his face.

"Knocks 'em dead," he said, shrugging.

"Serious?"

"You should try it."

The cop flashed the light along the dashboard, to the one silver can. He held the light there, looked at William.

"Do I need to check your license, sir?" he asked.

"It's old," William said, then took a chance, dropped one hand into shadow and leaned over to the window, as if reaching for his wallet. "But if you want. . . ?"

The cop started to step closer, breathed in the puppy shit again, and gagged, stepped out into the highway, and, without even thinking about it, William reached out through the window, pulled him back over, a Kenworth sucking past, its chrome mirror nearly skimming the camper shell, rocking the truck.

The cop tried to breathe, couldn't.

There was blood on his sleeve, now, from William's hand. On the black fabric.

He finally sucked in enough air to talk. His eyes wet, swimming.

"I know you," he said, leaning on the truck, watching the road behind his cruiser.

"The bear," William said.

The cop nodded.

"Whatever happened to it?" William said.

The cop lifted his head at the interstate, the truckers. "Them," he said, his lips already thinning. "It must have been alive, crawled back up there for one more round or some shit."

William nodded, leaned over to spit. The cop almost stepped back to let him, then just moved a little farther along the side of the truck instead.

It was all William could do not to smile.

The cop felt it too, just at the corners of his mouth, then patted William on the arm, told him to be safe, and extended his hand for a shake. But the twelve-inch light was still in it. Still on. And then he held it there.

William followed the pale beam.

Maybe sixty feet out, where the light started scattering into motes, was a tall black dog, her teats heavy with milk.

She was staring back along the beam of light.

The cop hissed through his teeth then took the light back, and told William to be safe. William nodded, watched the cop in the mirror, feeling along the side of the truck then disappearing behind it, walking as far in the ditch as he could back to his cruiser. Crawling in the passenger side.

He rolled the lights across his bar once in farewell, accelerated evenly into the night.

Minutes after he was gone, William pulled his headlights back on.

The dog was still there, watching him.

"Okay then, little momma," William said, and started easing the Chevy forward.

* * *

She was another sign, led him first onto the service road then to a copse of trees. Buried in the trees was a trailer house, burned out. The same one.

William shook his head no, no, that you don't do this, you don't *ever* come back to the same place, even if it's a perfect place, but she wasn't listening, had already lowered herself under the trailer's torn skirt.

He backed the Chevy to where he'd backed over Marissa's head three times. There were ruts from it almost—a shallow depression, like the earth remembered.

No lights, no nothing.

Just fast. It had to be fast.

But not like before, either. Not like when something had been watching from the front door of the trailer.

In six trips, William carried in the four dead dogs, the armful of puppies, and Julia. She was still breathing, but it was like she was having to remind herself to.

William nodded, kept nodding, and rested her down onto the mildewed couch. The dogs were already on the floor, the Shepherd's head lolling most of the way off, both ears still alert. A sorry state of affairs, but William would make do. He always had.

The seventh trip he made was for a six-pack of beer.

He stood over the hole where the sink had been and drank them one by one, dropping his cans down into the cabinet then digging them out to wipe his prints off. Walking back and forth from the Shepherd on the floor. Trying to fit the head back on. Telling himself it wasn't important but then caping it out some anyway, like a trophy. Reaching up into the skull to drag more out, enough that a section of leg might fit up there now. Always room for more.

He was on the fifth beer, breathing hard, almost ready, telling himself he didn't have time for Julia anymore but rubbing himself all the same, when one of the puppies rolled into her couch and he understood the whole, stupid night: the mother dog under the trailer, she was the one from the pound. The one whose puppies had been taken away. They'd killed her but she'd lived through it, and now here he was, with a whole, starving litter of ghost pups.

William smiled, left the beer half full on the counter.

He stepped down from the front door, off the wood somebody had stacked up as a staircase, and lowered himself to look under the skirt, snapped his fingers for her to come. She wouldn't, though. Wouldn't even growl, didn't care about whistles or promises.

William stood, not mad. Not anything, really.

"Julia," he called through the front door, sing-song, "Julia, I think she's hungry, dear," then stepped up, cut a perfect coin of meat from the palm of her right hand. Like a slice of pepperoni. He stood and her hand closed over the pain, and he thanked her, really meant it.

Down at the skirt again, he held the coin of meat into the darkness, but still the little momma wouldn't come, even when he left it there. So he kicked the trailer and hit it and spit on it. When he lowered himself to the skirt again, though, the coin was gone, and he smiled.

She understood.

William nodded, tuned in for a moment to a recap flapping on the interstate; his radio, leaking country music; his beer on the counter inside, fizzing down.

This was going to be even better, this was the next thing: before, he'd just been putting the girls *in* the dogs. Now, though—now he could feed them *to* the dogs. Julia, at least. And then, and then she could nurse the puppy he chose, and in that way it would be a perfect circle.

William knew he was rubbing himself again but couldn't help it, this was so good.

But then the skirt of the trailer, the very edge of the tin, dipped down into the surface of the ground.

William cocked his head to the side, not getting it, then followed the skirt up to the trailer, then to the door. The perfect pair of caramel legs there. The one breast pointing out into the night.

"Julia," he said, in his other voice, "I was just about to—" and then saw all the way up her, and fell back, never felt the ground.

It was Julia, but not. Julia, naked but for blood. Julia, with the dog head that had lolled off. The Shepherd. She'd pulled it down over her own somehow.

William felt his breath tremor in his chest, tried to smile, couldn't come close.

"Julia," he said again, and then she was stepping down, the black dog under the trailer exploding from the darkness, the square-headed grey puppies spilling around Julia's feet, down the rotten steps.

William pushed himself back through the dirt, tried to laugh at himself, at this, at her. Her gone-breast was leaking down her body, the fingers of the hand he'd cut the coin from dripping black. The eyes of the dog head watching him like a god, unblinking.

William laughed through his nose, wiped his eyes, and shook his head no to her now.

She had a hand to each side of the door jamb, was stepping down.

Laughing with no sound, William slashed the air with his razor but it was weak, nothing.

She lowered herself from the doorway to the dirt, leading with her good foot, the placement so deliberate that William suddenly felt what was happening here. Why. That it was time. That, after sixteen, seventeen girls, it was time. He nodded his head to her—*yes, yes, this*. He was ready.

"Please," he said to her, lifting his chin so she could have his throat, "please, I'm sorry," and then the dog head looked down at him with its dry eyes, knew him all at once, saw him in his cowboy hat, hiding in all the cushions of the couch, and he started throwing up down his chest, pushing back again, away from her, from it, and the body that had been Julia took one more step, no doorway to lean on now, and folded over the bad foot. Onto William. Her warm breath on his inner thigh, through the denim. The dog head nosing into his navel. William's whole body trembling, neck jerking, cheek stubble wet with tears.

He was alive.

She had spared him. She was forgiving him.

He breathed in, out, made a sound with his voice just to see if he still could. Felt his own nipples swelling with a sort of milk he could feed her with if she wanted.

Everything made sense.

Except then she growled.

From the Shepherd's mouth.

Instead of standing up like the woman she'd been, she pushed up onto her bowing-out arms, raised her heavy head to study him. To taste the air for him.

William kicked out from under her and she stayed crouched like that, on all fours. The Shepherd head just watching him.

"No, no, no," William said to it quietly, and the little momma dog under the trailer snarled back there in her wet darkness, and the puppies boiling in the doorway screamed with the voices of sixteen women, and William drew a sharp line across his left nipple with the razor, his own fluids spilling down his front, into his lap, in offering.

She just stared at him.

"Julia?" William said.

In reply, she took her first step, her right arm reaching out for the ground.

William pushed back farther, still shaking his head no, and a second before she lunged forward off her hind legs, he was turned, crawling into a blind run.

Billy Billy Billy the Kid, she said in his head, in her dog voice, and William leaned forward, deeper into the night, and the puppies and the trailer and his truck fell away behind them, and the one time William looked back, Julia's new mouth was moving, her teeth shiny wet and curving in and in, and this isn't one of those stories where the killer is chased by his own guilt out into the road to get run down by a truck his father could be driving, it's one of those stories where you understand that no matter how fast a man runs, a dog can run faster. Especially when she's hungry.

NO TAKEBACKS

1.

We didn't build the app to kill anybody.

It wasn't even our idea to build it, exactly. One day RJ's dad was just standing there in the kitchen with us after his work, and he pretty much foisted the idea on us. His tie was two-fingers loose and he was digging in the refrigerator for a beer. RJ and me were sitting on the island (me) and the counter (him), texting. Or, if I'm going to be honest here, for the first time in somewhat-recorded history, we were *pretending* to text.

That beer, RJ's dad was sure, had been there this morning? Yeah.

Anyway, he finally settled on some orange juice straight from the carton, and then he was just standing there with us like I said, doing that thing where he thinks we're all hanging out, being cool. At least he tries, though, right? More than I can say for my dad, who runs the house like a military barracks, telling us when we can and can't be at ease, soldiers. Interrogating me about my plans for the future if he ever finds me just sitting on the counter one fine lazy summer day.

To be specific, and blip back to RJ's kitchen, the *last* fine lazy summer day before senior year started.

"So . . ." RJ's dad said, wiping the extra-pulpy orange juice from his top lip, "what are you two troublemakers brewing up this particular afternoon, now?"

I didn't look up, couldn't, was too busy processing his 'brewing' and what it might or might not mean. Whether it was some kind of coded approval or explicit accusation or what.

"You know," RJ answered for both of us, shrugging to make it stick.

RJ's dad nodded, took another deep glug, and then asked if we had that red light, green light one yet?

We looked up to him with reptile eyes.

"That *app*," he said, about the phones we were still working, and his eyes, they were all glittery with possibility.

I did a short little mental groan, here. Kind of squinted in anticipation. Talking software outside your age group always feels like trying to use sign language through the bars of the gorilla cage.

"It's free, see," RJ's dad went on, "this computer kid from Palmdale, he made it for his little sister one afternoon, because he was supposed to be babysitting her but wanted to play online or something. There's an article in the paper today, yeah?"

"The paper," RJ repeated, his sentence the blade on some construction tractor, scraping bottom.

His dad was impervious, though. Had too much momentum. Was probably going to say 'computer kid' again, even.

"All you do is stop moving the phone when the light goes red, then on green light you—"

"Cool," I said, sliding down from the island. "Red light, green light, right?"

I pretended to be calling it up on my phone. On the way out.

"Not really," RJ's dad said, his tone downshifting a bit. "But that's not the point. The point is that that app, it's the new babysitter. All the parents are downloading it for their babies now. Three hundred thousand so far. And counting."

He let that hang.

"Dollars?" RJ finally asked.

"Downloads," his dad said, licking his lips, excited. "And you know what? Each one of those downloads has his name on it. That afternoon watching his little sister, it got him into MIT, yeah? *Full ride.*"

"Ah, the Ride . . ." RJ said, sliding down from the counter now as well.

This was where all of his dad's casual just-hanging-out stories always ended up: some kid getting a full ride to college.

But still.

Three hundred thousand downloads? With how many screen refreshes per session?

Probably a million impressions, easy.

And even at a tenth of a cent per—you could do some serious bank that way.

All we needed now was the app.

RJ's great idea was "Naked Leapfrog." I wasn't against it, especially as it involved asking Lindsay from Chem to help, but when my mom found our storyboards on the kitchen table that night, we had to have another sit-down with my dad when his shift was up at ten.

It went the usual way.

The only reason I got to keep my phone was by arguing that I was testing code on it, for my college applications.

RJ chimed in too, and threw in a Corvette if the app really took off, if my dad was interested in looking cool.

"A *sports* car," my dad said, and leaned back in what he called his Spartan chair. His no-nonsense chair.

RJ shrugged, the left side of his mouth eeking over a bit, and, as it turned out for the next twenty minutes, my dad actually had a thought or two about sports cars. Complete with anecdotes and horror stories and statistics. There was maybe even some kind of insurance quote in there.

I apologized to RJ with what of my face I could—we've been friends since third grade, so he got it—and then, slouching across the dark driveway to recompose ourselves in the bushes (one cigarette, maybe two), ash out on RJ's old dog's real headstone again, RJ said, "Dude, if only we could have seen *that* one in the rearview," and I kind of looked behind us, had to agree.

People have gotten rich on worse ideas.

Most of what we needed for the app we could scavenge from stuff already on the market, though a couple of those took enough hours to crack that night that we probably should have just written them ourselves.

"And we can't ask Lindsay?" RJ said, his game keyboard glowing up his face like this was a campfire story we were telling to each other, conditional by conditional, curly bracket by curly bracket.

"She'll be all over us once the cash is rolling in," I told him.

We hunched back to the coding.

The app we were building was going to be the definition of elegance. Just because it was so simple, or could be, if we wrote it straight. Not a game, not some stupid trivia, no overlooked system utility or navigation aid for amateur seamstresses, and definitely not another porn scrubber or privacy screen.

A camera.

Just that.

It wasn't supposed to kill us.

* * *

What our app would have going for it was what RJ called the 'chill factor.' It was what he'd wanted to call the thing, even—nobody else was using it for an app yet—but I talked him down from that particular ledge, pulled us back to the realm of the sane: 'No Takebacks.' Even though takebacks was pretty much exactly what our app was about.

RJ's complaint about wishing we'd seen my dad's Corvette lecture coming? We were marrying that to a handheld device, then, if everything panned out, amping it up into a portable haunted house.

The idea was that, when you had that feeling somebody was behind you, just kind of lurking, waiting—Simms in Marketing taught us this last year: find something everybody alive shares, then winnow that down to a product they can buy—when you had that feeling, you could just 'check your messages' or whatever (this is you, calling the app up) then lower your hand back down, the phone still palmed there, and snap a pic of the world directly behind you.

Which you could already do, sure—the problem with global anxieties is that there's usually a global fix already in place—especially if you had the know-how to re-assign your shutter to a mechanical button. But, as we tested and found, it took some pretty serious skill and no small amount of dumb luck to keep that camera straight up and down. Pushing that mech button, it turned out it wasn't just your finger muscles that got involved. Your whole hand tensed up, whether you told it to or not, and right at the wrong moment: when you were pushing the button.

If you hack into the image stabilization routines and crank them up, they can scrub most of that motion out, yeah. But that just leaves you with a fairly clear shot of whatever you've got in the frame. Which is to say that, when you're not looking, your aim tends to be off. Big surprise, I know. It turned out we were real good at snapping pics of the floor or the ceiling or our own asses, but hardly ever got what was behind us lined up properly.

Our revolutionary solution, then, was to hook a line or two of code between the phone's gyroscope and the camera's shutter, so that the image would only capture when the phone was straight up and down, perfectly vertical, giving it a straight look back.

As for lateral, though, the side-to-side—well, the app was going to be free, right? The only thing that could correct for that would be . . . a bluetooth tie-in with a near-eye device strung up like a periscope? some infrared sensor to square the phone with the room? a fisheye lens? We could fake the fish-eye trick anyway, just stretch the image, let it distort out, but that wouldn't change the original field of view, would just suggest it had been wider than it was, and the market was already spilling over with this kind of sleight-of-hand tomfoolery.

Finally we just stole another of RJ's dad's garage beers, smuggled it to the bushes, toasted Cedric (the dead, headstoned dog), and started in with the field trials.

The app worked perfectly. Better than we could have dreamed. A thousand people should have thought of this already.

We took turns trying to sneak up on each other, caught ourselves on film each time, without having to look back. And it was good we ran the tests, too, or we never would have figured out to make the flash optional, and, in case there were some legacy phones out there not playing the game (ours did), we fiddled with the autorotate, to keep the image from getting flipped, because, when you're trying to catch some slender dude ghosting up behind you, you don't need to be worried about if you're phone's upside down or not.

The lateral still sucked, of course, but what we'd lucked into there was that, when the washed-out, black-and-whited image of us playing backdoor ninja was only *half* in the image, it was approximately eighty-*five* times creepier.

Score one for the good guys.

So we went back to the drawing board (RJ's basement room, the door locked), put a fat-fingered toggle on the flash, dialed up the contrast some, and then spent the rest of our last before-school weekend trancing on how to layer in random pics from the phone's gallery, the same way those 'zombie yourself' apps stenciled gore over your face.

The difference there, though, was that those apps were more participatory, always asked you to position your face in the dotted green lines, please, and, even with that kind of help, still, the final image kind of sucked.

The other problem was the random pics being sucked from the phone's gallery. What if, instead of a snap of your mom cooking hamburgers—we'd just copy her outline over, fill the rest with textured shadow—what if what the app sucked across to pretend was sneaking up behind you, what if it was a pretty sunset, an idyllic windmill?

So we killed hours and many many braincells coming up with just five stock images to bundle in with the app: a girl crawling on the 'wall,' a guy just standing there, a hand starting to reach around some corner, a pair of floating eye smudges, and a simple wisp of smoke you could take to be whatever you wanted, or didn't want. And we figured how to fade them into these 'take-back' shots like they'd been there all along. It was spooky as hell.

Except.

One thing you learn, coding, is that there's always an 'except.'

It was RJ who stumbled onto it: when you download those stupid rotating wallpaper apps or one of those 'innocent maze with a jack-in-the-box zombie' numbers, there's always that download lag, where the server's sneaking those hidden images across. It wasn't so much that we were worried about people watching the progress bar, keeping a close eye on the running printout right above it—we *would*, but that was us—it was that, sneaking stuff into somebody's memory like that, caching it they-don't-know where, that was a porn move. And even if it was just a machine reviewing our app, not a real person, still, that kind of underhandedness, even if it was all in good fun: we were going to get filtered.

Never mind that, after our app cycled through all five *sneak_up* images, the joke's tired, the app deleted, only rated on how it ended, not how it was.

We stole another beer, considered things.

No, a windmill wasn't scary, even if it was three foot high and sneaking up behind you in the hall.

No, it wasn't scary to see that same girl crawling along the side of the hall.

What we finally settled on, though it was going to slow the process down, was upping the array of stock images from five to a cool hundred, and rigging the recursion such that it would iterate through however many images we made available, really. We were in it for the long haul, after all, and RJ was a serious whiz with fake randomnocity, and me, my job was to strip each of these images down to the bare bones. My goal was to get each down to about five kilobytes, but the wall I ran into was, of course, pixelation, which, unless you're somehow in the game, isn't all that scary. So what I finally lucked onto was letting the images swell back up to a whole fifteen kilobytes—they were all greyscale, had some definite blur built-in—but *then* just scaling them down to micro. Bam: seven kilobytes per, about. We had to dial the smoothing up a bit to compensate, but all in all, it was working.

All that was left was to push these little *sneak_up* images into some buried directory online, .htaccess it for all time (though 'Lindsay' could probably break in . . .), and we were on to the second round of trials.

The app was light, it didn't glitch, it had a hooky name, some promised fun, and we'd left some space at the bottom of each image for all the banners that were going to run.

"So?" RJ said, standing up from his bed.

"It's Sunday night," I told him.

Our eyes were bloodshot, our fingertips raw, our pores were exhaling cheese puffs—another weekend gone, lost forever between two curly brackets no one would ever properly appreciate.

But it had been worth it, too.

Screw college, right?

RJ walked me across his driveway, my dad's security light popping on as soon as we stepped up onto the concrete.

The app was on both our phones, of course, and our laptops too.

"Don't take any pictures I wouldn't," RJ said, stopping at the free-throw line to sail an imaginary one in, and I saluted him, spun slow and fake-drunk on my heels—just another sailor, looking for my gangplank home—and leaned into whatever my dad had waiting for me after not checking in all weekend again.

Tomorrow was the first day of senior year, though.

There was nothing he could do to me that would matter.

2.

By Wednesday, RJ was a ghost.

Not literally (not yet), but that was kind of just his place in the cafeteria, in the halls, in the parking lot.

Usually, I'd be right there with him, but somehow the Life Sciences I was having to make up from sophomore year, it had taken off. Mostly because I wasn't the only one having to make it up.

Lindsay was in there too. My new lab partner.

It was taking me longer and longer to get ready each morning. My dad would grumble over the breakfast table about the girl I was becoming, and how pretty I was getting, and I'd just chew, swallow, and float to second period again.

I'd like to say I had no illusions about Lindsay and me, about homecoming and prom and life, but it went way past that. I was neck-deep in that particular fantasy, and sinking fast.

At lunch I found RJ, leaned in, told him my plan.

"*Her?*" he said back.

Her phone was newer, brighter, better, was supposed to be harder to hack. I wanted to try the app there, if she was game.

"Maybe we'll play some Naked Leapfrog too," I told him, shrugging, trying to come off more lecherous than I was.

"I put a text button on it," RJ said back.

"Link-with-attachment, right?" I said, suddenly concerned.

He didn't dignify that.

Of course it would be link-with-attachment. Trying to build our own cute little text program *inside* our app, we'd have to be poring through different carriers' protocols, asking permission for this, not stepping on that.

"What about the Lonely Brigade?" I asked.

It was our code for the social networks.

"You think?" he said, kind of doing his sneer thing.

We were really talking now. Like it had always been.

"Why not?" I said. "That's where we want the pics to show up, don't we?"

"There's no revenue for second-hand impressions," he said. "You know that, right?"

Because there would be no real way to track them.

"But we can brand them, anyway," I said. "Just clear-letter, discrete. Directing them back to the app, keeping it part of the chain, all that." RJ shrugged one shoulder, was watching somebody across the cafeteria.

It was Lindsay. I could tell by the way he let his eyes keep skating past her.

"Remember that toddler game?" he said, coming back to me. "That my dad said?"

"Red light, green light. Go directly to college."

"That's all he could use it for, wasn't it? For his MIT application. Because—putting banners on it would be stupid, wouldn't it? Who advertises to babies?"

I blinked, focused.

He was right again.

"But we're not like that," I said.

He shook his head no, agreeing with me.

But still.

That guy, that app, he was our origin story. And now it was hollow. Now he was somebody we'd make fun of.

"Think the app'll scare her?" he asked then, catching my eyes for a flash.

"You sleeping, man?" I asked back.

"Jump right out of her pants, right?" he went on, then lifted his chin to get me to look.

It was Lindsay, maybe two steps from us, balancing her water-with-lemon, her salad.

She smiled, twirled past, biting her lip in hello and doing something impossible with her eyebrows.

"Life Science," RJ said, *not* watching her walk away. "What's homework going to be like for that, you think?"

"Exactly," I said, and brushed past him, my eyes glued.

Two days later, RJ started texting me some of the new takeback images he was generating.

I was in the library with Lindsay and two of her friends. But mostly with Lindsay. At least in my head.

So far I'd agreed to show her where she could nab papers online, places the faculty didn't know about. I was going to show her where all the good music and movies were, too, but was going to space it out some. Surprise her on Thursday with what wasn't in the theatres until Friday, that kind of stuff.

You use what you've got, I mean. This was my one chance.

And now RJ was helping.

I looked at the image he'd flashed across, then lowered it under the table, scanned both ways to see if any teachers were close.

"What?" Lindsay said.

Her dad wouldn't let her load any apps he didn't scan first, as it turned out. The human virus checker, as it were.

But when you've got a daughter like that.

"Give me your number," I said to her—that easy—and bank-shot the image off a tower two miles a way, drilled it back under the table, to her phone, balanced right there on her thighs.

It was a takeback pic, sure, but RJ had done something different, had twisted the code back on itself somehow.

Behind the washed-out version of his long hallway was the crawling girl. She wasn't on the wall anymore, though, but the floor. And not floating two feet above it like could happen, but right on the surface of the carpet, reaching forward along it like a cat, her face just blank.

Lindsay dropped her phone. It rattled under the table.

More, I texted back to RJ.

We were going to be so rich.

I thought that was the only way things could go, yeah. There's going to be an empty seat at graduation now, though.

Maybe two.

By the beginning of the next week, RJ was a star, at least on the cell networks. Instead of a ghost, now he was dragging a fuse. Like he'd weighed his options, studied the landscape of his life, considered the future, and made the measured decision that senior year, we were all going to know his name. One way or the other.

Let me say here that I never took credit for the images he was getting the app to produce.

I'd had a hand in the initial program, had spent a hurried two hours parsing through the code with him on Saturday, his dad grilling steaks for us in the backyard, but that was just maintenance and bugkilling, trying to get it all to spec before we took it live.

Before we could do that, though, we had to nab a domain—it was actually available, and, because it was for 'college,' his dad floated us twenty-four months on his card, base package—we had to stake out some freebie bulletin board, complete with set-up and FAQ threads, each of us set up as boss moderators. We were also supposed to write up little backstories for ourselves, to attach faces to the app.

"If you have time, I mean," RJ had said from behind his laptop, about that.

It was like we were playing battleship.

"Ha ha," I said back, and never looked up.

"So is this the end of our summer romance?" he said back, and this stopped me.

I looked around my screen, was about to say something back—no idea what, but I could feel the words in my throat—when his dad ducked in with news about those steaks, how if you don't pay at least glancing attention to the corporeal, then you risk getting lost forever in the abstract—his usual out-loud bumpersticker—and I forgot what RJ had said.

That night it came back, though.

Two-thirty in the morning found me at our living room window, no lights on behind me, to give away that I was there.

In the bushes there was the cherry of a cigarette, rhythmic like a heartbeat. Except slower. More deliberate. And at the wrong height for RJ.

Unless he was breaking his own rules, using Cedric's custom little headstone as a bench.

He was.

I hugged my arms to my sides, felt the coldness of my phone press into my bare skin.

Without looking back, I glowed the phone on, opened the app, and lowered my hand, the picture snapping once the phone was straight up-and-down enough.

The picture was empty, of course.

Just our couch, that stupid floor lamp I used to think was a robber. The doorway to the left of it, black and yawning.

I deleted it.

Probably the scariest image RJ sent to me that week, that he fully knew I had to show to Lindsay, who was going to cc the whole class, it was one of his dad that he'd doctored.

It was in the hall again, like the rest—my guess is he was using his mom's tall mirror at the turn into the living room to orient, keep the lateral in check—but it was different in that it was just static.

Over our cheese-puffed, brainstormy weekend, we'd agreed that the suggestion of motion, of something approaching the phone, that that was all *kinds* of scary. Better than something you were walking away from, anyway.

But this one, this time, it was what he was walking away from.

It was his dad, way back by his bedroom—RJ's mom's long gone, of course; I don't even remember her, so much—and he was just sitting against that wall, his legs splayed out in front of him, his head cocked over, an obvious kind of stain on the wall.

Lindsay looked up to me in Life Science when she saw it, and I looked away, wasn't thinking about money so much anymore.

That afternoon, I found reasons to be outside, stayed there just piddling until RJ's dad pulled up, lifted his briefcase to me on his way in.

I waved back, looked back to my house, and went inside to check if RJ had uploaded that particular shot to the hidden directory.

He hadn't.

It was just the stock hundred we'd come up with together. They seemed so tame now.

I was about to back out of that terminal—already had, really, had to key back in—when I caught the tail-end of that list of files I'd just called up.

The count was a hundred, like I'd been expecting, and they were named sequentially after the *sneak_up* lead-ins—clever clever—but there was another directory there now. *Inside* the protected directory.

I tried "Lindsay" as password, but it wasn't her this time.

I tabbed up, then, went root to try to at least see how many characters this password might have, but I suck in the shell, and the architecture, it was all different now, was some kind of chutes and ladders game, a labyrinth, one with dead ends and bottomless wells and something that, when I tried to open it, locked up my system.

What had RJ done?

I rebooted, was about to just rush that file system, hit it with everything I had, but then that image of RJ's dad was in my head again.

The bedroom door. The door to RJ's dad's bedroom.

I pulled my phone, called the picture up.

The doorway was on the wrong side.

Wasn't it?

Yes. I'd practically grown up over there. RJ's dad had encouraged it, even, after his last encounter with my dad.

But how could it be on the wrong side?

I stood, walked out into our own hall. It wasn't as long as RJ's, and had tables and junk all cluttered in it, but still.

I stood at the end, right by my doorway, closed my eyes and took a takeback pic.

Just normal.

I looked through the walls, to the memory of RJ's house, and then to this hall.

The mirror.

He had the mirror.

I dragged my mom's in from her closet—she was out walking, like always, 'because it was daylight'—set it up against the turn into the living room.

Already I didn't like this.

I could see myself too well. Like I was at the end of the hall, waiting for myself.

But screw it.

This wasn't for me, this was for the app. This was for RJ.

I walked up to my reflection, held my phone down and backwards, snapped another pic.

Nothing. Just the usual.

I turned around, sure I was missing something—did RJ's dad have some old brown-and-white photographs framed on the wall on the left side?—and lowered my phone, didn't realize the app was still on until I felt the camera burr, the image processing.

I held it up.

It was my hall, reversed.

Except I was standing there right in the middle of it.

"What are you doing?" I said out loud, to RJ, and just then my dad stepped into the hall in his workshirt, looked from the mirror to me and didn't even say anything. Just brushed past, shut his door behind him.

The day Lindsay gave me a ride home was the day RJ had to spend in the main office. There were counselors and principals and even a city police.

It wasn't for the takeback shot in circulation today—a benign old image of Cedric he'd blacked-out, let bleed at the edges, like he was loping up behind, his mouth glittering—but for the one of his dad, shot in the head.

"What do you think they'll do to him?" Lindsay said, both hands on the wheel.

"He's just screwing around," I told her.

Still, the support forum on our site had a few members now. From school, mostly, because he'd put the brand on the bottom of the images he was texting.

When Lindsay pulled up to my curb, I didn't get out at first.

I turned to her, was in some level of prep for asking her to maybe hold back on forwarding any more of the messages, that I needed to talk to RJ first, but then her face was right there.

I bumped into her, pulled back smiling.

And then we sort of kissed.

I rose from the car, drifted across the lawn, and, once the front door was closed my dad clapped me on the shoulder and then shook my whole body. It was in congratulations.

"A real piece," he said, my mom standing right there in the kitchen doorway, "you need any, you know, any—" but I was already in my room by then.

That night I trolled through our hidden directory again, was going to crack into that Area 51 if I had to use a crowbar, but then there was a new version of the app waiting right there, shuffled in with the images.

I put it on my phone, laid back on my bed so there'd be nothing behind me, and clicked through.

All that was different was the theme. We'd had it just standard silver and blue, tried and true, but now all the backgrounds were shades of black, and all the words—there weren't many— were a deep maroon.

The update log in the readme said that it had been blacked out for night use. So that the glow from the screen wouldn't give you away.

I looked to the front of the house. To me, standing in the

window, looking into my phone's bright display, having to squint from it after studying RJ in the bushes for so long.

The next day he was back in the halls, no problem.

The first text he sent explained that he was having to throttle back for the moment. So it was going to be dead dog pictures for the foreseeable future.

That's a complicated word to text, too, 'foreseeable.'

The attached image was another Cedric snap, in the same backwards hall, his toothless old mouth glinting in the washed-out sixty-watt.

He was closer now.

"How are you cloaking yourself?" I asked him, finally.

We were in the bushes, standing on a bed of cigarette butts.

Our beers were balanced on the headstone. RJ had carried them right out the front door.

"How am I what?" he asked back, squinting through the smoke.

"You're using the mirror," I told him.

He cocked his head over, said, "That one?"

We stepped out of the bushes and he hit his flashlight widget.

His mom's ancient old mirror was leaned up against the side of the house.

"It was sucking the light away," he said, then leaned back to the headstone.

"Your dad throw a fit?" I asked. Because his dad always did, when it came to his mom's things.

"I told him it was scaring me," RJ said, pinching his cigarette away like a tough guy, grinding it out on the bottom of his shoe. "Why, you want it?"

I looked out to the black monolith of his house, not a single light on.

Four hours ago, his dad had got back from work for the ten-thousandth time.

I shook my head no, I didn't want it.

"So we ready to go live then?" he said.

"Sure," I told him. "Whatever."

He nodded cool, we touched beer cans, and then he was gone, back to it, and I was still standing there when my phone got a text.

Lindsay, probably. Test tomorrow.

I was half right.

It was a long shot, blurry, from a made-up number, but still, you could just make out the two of us in her car, her mouth pressed against mine in the daylight, right there by the trash-cans and the mailboxes, where RJ and me had used to build big complicated ramps to launch our bikes up into the sky.

Only one of us came down, though.

I'm sorry, RJ.

Two days later, two days before it happened, Lindsay edged down beside me before Life Science, tipped her laptop over so I could scope it.

It was the bulletin board site. Mine and RJ's support thread, the FAQ, the bio of the app, all our best guesses at marketing.

"It's just for college," I told her.

"No, look," she said.

There was a new thread. It was the series of Cedric pics, like, if you glued them to the corner of a tablet of paper then flipped through them, you could see him creaking along again.

It was the next step.

Our pie-in-the-sky idea with the app, it had been to take not one shot, but five or six in a burst, then plant the same *sneak_up* image into each, a little closer, a little bigger, and *then*, when the user opened that file, thinking they were just getting a static pic, they'd instead get an image that all of the sudden stuttered ahead, so much closer to them.

That was the pay version, of course. Because you've got to have a pay version.

But now RJ was giving it away for free.

"No, this," Lindsay said, and scrolled down.

It was some kind of blog, or a long post.

No: the bios we were supposed to be attaching. The faces behind the app.

I don't remember RJ's exactly, word-for-word, and it's gone now, of course, is evidence in some file cabinet, has been scrubbed from the net, but I wouldn't want to remember it in that much detail, either.

Because RJ couldn't scare us with pictures anymore, what with everybody watching, he was using words, now. Trying to come up with a story to explain why Cedric was dogging him like that.

It wasn't even close to how it went down, though, the Cedric thing.

I mean, I had been there for it, kind of. It was right after RJ had moved in beside us, when his mom was still around.

Then one day, maybe after they'd unpacked their last box, she just wasn't. Even though her car keys were on the hook, her shoes in their place, her sunglasses (it was summer) by the sink. There was never any note, any ATM photo, any goodbyes.

In the middle of it all, too, when everybody in the neighborhood was volunteering their house to be searched—except my dad, of course, who knew his rights, and didn't so much need the law knowing about his gun collection—in the middle of all that, Cedric had turned up dead.

It was bad timing, but he was old, so it made a sort of sense, everybody guessed. Especially if he was grieving.

What didn't make sense—to my dad, at least—was the granite mini-headstone RJ's dad came home with. For the *dog*. After his wife had already obviously split with the vacuum cleaner salesman. But—this is still my dad—anybody who'd commemorate an animal like that, maybe his wife was just being reasonable, right?

And I'd never even once seen a vacuum cleaner salesman.

And, the whole thing—Cedric, RJ's mom—that whole first impossible year of craziness, of running to the door every time it rang, of buying longer and longer cords for the phone, it was never something RJ and me talked about. How do you, right? Still, that was where we met, right there at that dog funeral, so it's not like we could forget it either. My mom had walked me across to stand there with the new kid while RJ's dad droned on and on about the dog, really talking about his wife. Finally, I'd even cried, and RJ had edged over, stood close enough to me that we were kind of touching.

Ever since then, you know. Joined at the hip, all that. Battleship combatants for life.

But friendships forged over a dead pet, I guess they've got a built-in expiration date. This re-do RJ had spun up of what happened to Cedric, and just to sell a piece of software, just to make everybody in senior class finally notice him—it had to be over, me and him.

And Cedric was the tame part, too.

The real story was what had really happened to his mom that day, what the neighborhood had been waiting to find out for years. But RJ and his dad didn't even *have* a garbage disposal back then, I don't think. Maybe a therapist would see some kind of call or plea in what-all RJ made happen to her in his fake bio, I don't know. That doesn't mean he'd turn his back on RJ for even a moment, though.

According to the post, Cedric hadn't died of old age or, as RJ's dad wanted, of sadness either. His spirit wasn't out wherever RJ's mom was now, keeping her safe.

The way RJ had it, it was the rings that had killed Cedric. And the necklaces. The earrings. Three brooches, a handful of bracelets, because garbage disposals can't chew metal.

But neither could Cedric, so it had to be forced down with this little mini-Louisville Slugger he had. Piece after piece, all RJ's mom's jewelry. *A little internal bleeding for the family hound*—I remember that part. And not on purpose.

When I was done with it that first time, that only time, I shook my head no, my eyes wet, and pulled Lindsay's laptop shut as gently as I could, like I didn't want everybody to hear.

"Do you want to just sleep at my house?" she said, the worry there in her eyes. "My parents are, you know. This weekend."

I swallowed, tested my voice in my head before using it, asking if she wanted me to bring a movie, something like that.

"Can you get any, like, anything to drink, you think?" she said.

"You like beer?" I asked back, still not looking right at her but into the future.

Anything was possible.

3.

That afternoon—this was Friday, the Friday before the rest of my life—RJ opened their utility door, caught me at his dad's refrigerator, my arms clinking with garage beer.

"I'll pay you back," I told him.

"Remember Zelda?" he said back, not even a little concerned about the beer, or his dad.

"Which one?" I asked.

We'd raced through them all.

"Fourth grade," he said.

NES. His dad had insisted we start there, even though it had already been a serious antique by our third grade.

He was right, too. It was the right place to begin.

I got the last beer I could carry, balanced it on top and eased the refrigerator door shut with my calf.

"Gannon with two n's . . ." I said, then looked all the way up the steps to him. "So, this mean you're back, man?"

"Where have I been?" he said, something mocking in his voice.

"We need to take it live," I said, catching a beer, and he heard the goodbye in my tone, opened his hand for me to waltz out into whatever this night held for me, and started the garage door down before I was halfway across the drive.

Because I was suddenly sure that if I looked back, I'd see Cedric trotting up out of the past, barely going to make it under the door, I looked back, fumbled the one bottle that kept getting away. It shattered at my feet, the door sealed itself to the concrete, and I wanted so bad to scrape that brown glass over, into the little gutter RJ's dad always edged between the drive and the grass, then maybe get the hose to take care of the guilty smell. But Lindsay. Lindsay Lindsay Lindsay. And RJ's dad knew we were into that beer anyway, didn't he? He had to. It was understood.

Just before she picked me up, my dad surely driving home from his shift, his face grim as ever, his talk radio whispering to him—I was having to time this so perfect—my phone buzzed with a text.

It was the lamp in my living room, the image I'd deleted. It was just standing there. Different anonymous number.

I looked to RJ's house and the one light that was on, it went off.

Pulling away with Lindsay, then, we passed RJ's dad, and, right before she turned right for her house, I caught RJ's dad's brake lights flaring. So he wouldn't run over that shattered bottle on his concrete. So he could get out, be sure he was seeing what he was seeing. So he could walk inside, ask RJ what he knew about this, RJ looking up at him from his laptop, a tolerant grin already pasted on his face.

I shut my eyes, rubbed a cold beer against my face, and I'm sure it goes without saying here that, when we got to her place, her parents were gone like she'd said—that was never the part anybody lied about—but four of her friends *were* there, and they *had* brought movies.

They held their hands over the back of the couch for the beer, laughed and giggled, and I slept in Lindsay's little brother's bedroom, could at least say now that I had spent the night at

Lindsay's, even if it was in dinosaur sheets. But I walked home the next morning without waking any of them, telling myself in my head that this was part of it, that this is how you grow up, that you can't be a complete adult until you've acquired the requisite amount of shame, and all I was doing was placing one foot in front of the other, so that I heard that distinct little *pop* at nearly the exact moment I realized I'd just stepped up onto my driveway.

That pop, that shot, it had come from next door. From RJ's. It was the sound the counselors and principals and police had all seen coming, that they were probably all ready for.

I stepped back to the middle of our yard, could feel the parentheses forming around my eyes, the hole starting in my chest, in my life, and then, like he'd been listening for this to happen for nine years now, like he could already see RJ's dad slumping down against the wall by his bedroom, my dad straight-armed our door out, was walking down our flagstones with purpose.

Down along his right leg was the revolver he kept tucked into the seat of his no-nonsense chair.

In the bushes then, I heard something, a rustling, and my face prickled, my eyes caught on fire, and I knew as true as I've ever known anything that Cedric was about to push through, that his mouth was going to be bright with jewelry, and for a moment I even saw just that—the gold, splintering the early morning light—but then it was RJ, half his face dark with blown-back blood, his chest rising and falling, his dad's small pistol already raised, his pace quick behind it, like he'd told himself he couldn't do this, but maybe he could if he just walked really fast and pretended it was all a movie.

He was already pulling the trigger too, and it was soundless, or, all I could hear, it was all the women's rings he was wearing, clacking against the trigger guard.

The first shot hit our brick wall where the roses used to grow, and the second whipped into the grass by my right foot, and the third slapped into my dad's shoulder, spun him around a little, this sideways red plume hanging behind him now, just like a paintball that had gone all the way through somehow.

This had been coming too long for that to slow him down, though.

He was walking and shooting as well, pointing his gun like a finger at RJ, like it was some hard-earned truth he was telling him here. Like this lecture wasn't over yet, son.

They met on the oil-stained concrete of our driveway, almost gun-to-gun, and neither stopped until they were empty, and just before RJ slumped over, back into the bushes, the best parts of him spread all over my yard, he looked over to me like he was seeing me over Cedric's grave for the first time, seeing that he wasn't going to have do this alone after all, and I could see in his eyes that he was saving me, with this. From my dad. That our summer romance wasn't over yet.

And then the rest.

Our app, dead. Our web page, dead. RJ and my dad, dead. Cedric's grave empty. The school in mourning, extra counselors bussing in, news vans lurking. My mom getting a triangle flag she just put in the top of the closet. Somebody down at the grocery store saluting me so that I had to duck down an aisle I didn't even want.

Over, done with, gone, end of program, reboot.

Except.

Three days ago, thumbing through my app drawer, I lucked onto ours. The last version RJ had rigged, the black-backgrounded one, with the maroon letters so faint you had to kind of just trust they were there.

It was a terrible design. The old people would hate it.

It was going to go viral.

I'd never even tried it, though.

I hovered the pad of my thumb over it, knew I was going to light it up, that I had to, for RJ, that I owed him that, but then made the command decision that if I could see the scaffolding first, the haunted house wouldn't get to me.

I sucked the app onto my laptop, scrolled through the code, lost myself in the elegance again, the simplicity. The innocence, right? All it was was a camera with a different trigger, then a bit of post-capture image processing, a harmless call out to a hidden directory. It might get us into some school for marketing, but, as far as programming went, it was practically juvenile.

It might get *me* into marketing school, I meant.

And then I found RJ's last fix.

He'd commented it out, even, in case we wanted to go back. Our routine was, when combing each other's lines, the second one through would erase the notations as he went.

It meant this version, technically, it wasn't complete yet.

I arrowed my cursor up to his trailing escape slash, highlighted the whole note, inverting the text of the last thing he'd said in here . . . what? Two weeks ago? I unpacked his cryptic timestamp in my head. The first week of school, yeah. When I was in Life Science, getting a lab partner. I bit my lower lip in, shook my head. Who even timestamps their comments, right? RJ, that's who. He always did it, for—his words—*his* posterity's sake. And then he'd reach back into his pants, for his ass, and try to slap me on the shoulder, really rub his hand in.

I backspaced the comment, left the cursor blinking there at his new line, his last innovation.

All it did was pull a horizontal flip on the image. The easiest thing in the world.

It was why his hall had started turning up backwards. It was software, not the mirror, not the hardware.

I saved it, then saved it again to make it stick. The cursor just blinking up at me like I was being stupid here.

It was right.

But still—something didn't fit. It wasn't Area 51, either. Area 51 had been hidden in the *hidden* directory, and the hidden directory was gone, burned down by the police to keep sickos from leaving digital roses on its stoop.

At first I thought it was that one line of code—code that was explicitly just reversing whatever the camera had captured—it wasn't nearly enough to scrub RJ from the image, from the reflection he was backed up against to reverse his hall, but then I had to thump my temples with the heels of my hands: there *was* no mirror, idiot. Get off that horse already.

And then one of those moments of calmness hit me, where I could feel myself breathing, could feel the rasp of all those air molecules diving down my throat.

Yes.

I fumbled my phone up, my fingers shaking, and peeled through the texts he'd sent. The images. They were all in our forever-long thread. I snapped it off to give me a useable scrollbar and paged through, holding all those air molecules in now.

It couldn't be, though.

Each image, each snap he'd taken of that long hall behind him, each time, the lateral was perfect. The center of focus, the bullseye, it was that back wall where they'd found his dad. In every image, there was the exact same amount of wall on each side, like the perspective, it had to be perfect to tunnel through this.

Had he—had he cropped all the images, then loaded them back on his phone to blast to me and the rest of the senior class?

But, he would know that the same angle, the same positioning, that would kill the scare just the same as using the same five stock images.

Then it must mean he'd masking-taped around his feet on the carpet, stood in the exact same place each time, and, I don't know, used a magic marker on his mom's mirror, one that would match up with the back of his hand to get the phone in the same place time after time.

Except there was no mirror.

Stupid, stupid, stupid.

And even if he'd done that, still, it would take fifty images to get one that had the exact same angle as last time.

I was breathing hard now. Too hard.

Was he using one shot of the empty hall as backdrop to them all?

It was the only thing that made any kind of sense.

I dove into the code again, deeper than deep, looking for any routine that would allow sampling from the same background.

Nothing.

Of course he could have done it all on his laptop, right? To what purpose, though? He was more careful than that, would never make a background come off re-used and tired.

Then there was only one other option.

He'd cracked the side-to-side thing, just not commented it out. Or he'd lucked into it, maybe pasted one algorithm before instead of after another, so that it got first bite at the variables, and that had made all the difference.

There was nothing in the code, though, even when I used some ancient Perl to compare the old app to the new one.

Except for that one line, and the style junk with the colors, which was in the stylesheet anyway, they were the same.

I slammed the laptop, paced my room, pushed my phone against my forehead like I could force myself to think, here.

If you've never cried a bit from coding, then you've never really coded.

It goes the other way too, though.

The rush of cracking it, of cueing into the Beauty, the Truth, it's all the heroin any junkie could ever need.

And I was so close.

And RJ, he'd been there already, I could see that now. It was where all his calmness had come from. Take my dad's beer, it doesn't matter. Go with her. Let's take it live, infect the world with it.

I stopped pacing, stared into my phone.

That was it.

I was just looking at the scaffolding, was stuck behind the curtain. Maybe the key was in the product, though.

I touched the app, breathed life into it, and was going for the living room, to snap a takeback pic from the front window, see if it would lateral up with the one I'd taken before, but of course that one was gone, deleted once and then deleted again, when it showed back up, ha ha, RJ.

And the living room would probably be too big anyway.

Instead, I just stepped out of my bedroom, into the hall. It wasn't as long as RJ's, but it had to be the standard width. There had to *be* a standard width. Maybe that mattered.

I pulled my door shut, turned around to face it, lowered my phone to vertical and let the shutter snap.

Then I cocked my wrist forward, disturbing the gyroscope, and dropped it down straight again, the camera burring completion in my palm.

Of course.

I did it again, to be sure, and again.

We'd never built in a kill switch. I was going to have to go back in, release the gyroscope after the first pic. If I didn't, the processor would lag, trying to run post-production on a stack of polaroids.

You can't think of everything, though.

Before opening my door again, I checked behind me. Just to be sure.

Nothing.

I crashed on my bed, my back wedged into the corner like always, headphones cupping my ears, and checked the images.

They were empty.

I mean, my hall was there, and there was a smudge of disturbance at about chest-level, telling me something had tried to load in there. But it had aborted.

This is the way it goes, yeah. You duck in for a quick-fix, just to see how something works, and then nothing's working.

It was probably the banner's feed slot that was jacking with the fade-in, too. I was strict with always using all jpeg or all png or all gif in whatever I wrote, but RJ always said he could keep it straight, it's not like he was going to do something global with them all at once, right?

Except the app *was* doing something global with the array it was pulling from the hidden directory.

Oh, wait: the hidden directory that *wasn't there*.

Of course it couldn't load the images.

Still, the way we'd written it, there should have been a big distortion in the hall, not a small, unenlarged one. And, if this app was going to work, if it was going to generate revenue, then that banner needed to quit jacking with things.

And, because we didn't have sponsors yet, the banner RJ had dummied in, just to make sure it fit, it was Zelda. The old one.

It made me lean over, see if my NES console was still in the corner somewhere, tangled in its cords. Maybe one last turn through Hyrule would be the right send-off for RJ. The right thank you. Because—it's stupid, but we'd never really left it behind. That first day RJ's dad had mentioned red light, green light to us in the kitchen? Why I'd been the one sitting on the island, not RJ, it was because of Zelda. In the NES version he'd introduced me to in third grade, he'd always been fascinated with the boulders, with how, if you walked around some of them three times, then came back the other way, a door would open up.

For us in elementary, the same way the floor lamp in my living room had always been the robber, come to take me away, his kitchen island had always been our boulder. One time, spending the night, he even told me that's where his mom had really gone, he was pretty sure. That he had walked wrong to the refrigerator, gone back for the butter he'd forgot by the toaster, then gone back the other way around the island, made some secret door swing open in her closet, and she had just reached through, fallen the rest of the way.

It's stupid, but it's real. Or, it was to us.

"You shit," I said to him, just out loud, for making me think of all that again, but then . . . could that be it? This app *had* lived on RJ's rig at the end, after all. What if the little image-reverse he'd built in, what if that was Link, turning back to go the opposite way around the boulder now? What if the double-twist plus one necessary to open whatever door, what if it was just holding your phone upside down (1), backwards (2), and *then* flipping that image (3), which was already under so much strain just to stay straight?

That was just three things, though.

The boulders always required a fourth.

I checked my phone just before it shook in my hand, reminding me the images were ready—RJ's idea.

I scrolled through them, still empty, and then the phone shook again, which was one more time than we'd coded for. Had RJ sneaked a *reminder* vibration in as well? But where? It would be scary, though, like the app was insisting, was trying to warn the user.

But one thing at a time.

I slammed the pics onto my laptop to try to figure if that distortion in the air could help me diagnose things.

It didn't.

The scaled-back pictures that shouldn't have been there, as their directory had been burned—there they were, stacked on my desktop. I clicked the top one, had a bigger screen now, and could zoom, see that it was just the crawling girl, scaled back to bug-size, hanging there in the air of the hall, not even remotely scary.

"Are you local or what?" I asked the top one, and thumbed through my phone's cache.

No.

I wheeled the crawling girl close then far, close then far, like she was coming for me.

It wasn't scary.

Still, before getting back to the real work of the night—it was completely possible my phone had cached those hundred images in some way I was too tired to lock onto—I decided to make sure the sampling was truly random, anyway, wasn't just the first few from the array. Because that wouldn't be nearly so easy a fix. Cracking RJ's fake randomness, the 128 bit keys he liked to paste in, pretend he was hinging stuff on—it would be easier to just start over.

And maybe those keys were the source of the problem, even. Or the secret to keeping the lateral straight.

The top pic I'd already been seeing, of course. Crawling girl. Next was the shadow fingers we'd rigged reaching around a corner, but, just like all the *sneak_up* images in RJ's hall, the app had placed them perfectly somehow, right on the edge of the doorway opening onto the living room.

Maybe the width of the hall did matter.

I nodded, went to the next.

It was the smoke. Like a progression.

Maybe that was a good idea, too, if we ever did that fake animation on the paid version: sequence the stock images, build some logic in that wouldn't let this one pop unless that one had.

I clicked ahead, looking at my door instead of the screen for no real reason, and, when I came back to the laptop I felt a new hollowness in the deadspace behind my jaws, pushed the screen away so hard it shut.

My lungs were trying to hyperventilate or something.

No, my head, my *head* was doing that.

Same difference.

I looked to the door again. It was still shut.

I came back to the laptop, its side-light telling me it wasn't asleep yet, no. That it was waiting for me.

What I'd seen, what was there, it was—but it couldn't be.

A boy, about twelve. Washed-out and black and white. Skinny, shirtless, his pants just hanging off him.

RJ in sixth grade?

I wanted it be him, yes, because our summer romance wasn't over. Then *he* could be the fourth time around the boulder, right? The app only hits hyperdrive or whatever after satisfying 1, 2, 3, and a strange fourth, which, like Cedric had been for him, could be somebody close to you, dead. A blood sacrifice, to lubricate those doors that shouldn't open.

But it wasn't RJ.

RJ would never pull a lampshade over his head and stand there like that, just waiting for me to see him.

It was my dad when he was a kid. I knew. All his anger, his rules, his haircuts and talks, it was all there in the empty spaces between his ribs. The muscles that hadn't grown in. The bruises, the white lines of old cuts, burns above the sleeve lines.

I shook my head no, please, not him, not this.

Anybody but him.

But it couldn't be, either.

I was still being stupid, like with the mirror. Had to be.

I breathed down to a rate that didn't scream panic, watched my hand cross that bedspread space between me and the laptop, and opened it.

The image was gone, the hall empty again.

Was that worse or better, though?

"Mom?" I called out, then called again, louder, and then my phone shook in my hand again, stiffening that whole side of my body.

"No, no," I said to the phone, and only opened it because I was afraid it was going to ring if I didn't, which would definitely set me screaming, kickstart the kind of feedback loop I could never claw my way back from.

There was no image on my screen, no lampheaded boy.

Just the app, waiting, primed. Insisting.

I turned the phone around, to see the lens—maybe RJ had figured out how to sonar the flash to control the lateral?—and just when it got vertical enough, it snapped a takeback pic of me.

I dropped it again, but it was still plugged into my laptop.

The image resolved on my screen.

It was me, like it should have been, but behind me, instead of the glare of my wall, my posters, my bulletin board, there was all this open space. Years and years of emptiness to fall through.

And then the light on my ceiling fan sucked back into itself.

I opened my mouth to scream but before I could the bulb flashed back, dying, bathing the room in its fast blue light.

Standing at the end of my bed was the lampshade boy.

I straightened my legs, pushed back, away from him, and my phone rang. It was the single loudest thing ever.

I fumbled it up before its ringer could split the world in two, slammed it to the side of my head and, in her sleep voice, my mom asked if I'd been calling her, if I needed anything, where was I?

I tried to say something, to tell her, to tell her all of it, but, in the glow of my laptop screen, in the light from my phone, the room was empty again.

For now.

THE COMING OF NIGHT

At first you might consider them your competition, but as the week unfolds, they will more than likely become your last resort.

And you're not even certain they're real, is the thing.

But isn't that always the case?

Example: at the second bar, you noticed her because the bartender was ignoring her with the exact same level of contempt he was ignoring you. Because you were each nursing your drinks, trying to make them last. Using them in the same way a duck hunter might use a blind: to hide behind; to blend in. To go unnoticed.

Did she notice you as well, though?

You have to allow that. Underestimating your opposition, that's a thing you only ever get to do once.

So, though it made you physically ill, made you lurch to the bathroom, risk losing the thread of the night altogether, you ordered another drink, and another after that, and downed them in neat succession—not like you haven't made sacrifices before—even set the tumblers back onto the bar harder than necessary, to be sure she would tune in to your display.

Of course she couldn't be bothered.

But, if you were her, then you would feign the same nonchalance, wouldn't you?

It's complicated, being you.

Hypervigilance and indifference are two sides of the same coin, yet you have to show both at once. Sometimes while spilling yourself into a crusty public commode.

But nobody said it was going to be easy.

Wedge your foot against the bathroom door and clean the vomit from your lips, now, check your face from every angle to be sure. Maybe a linger, a touch, sure.

You're anybody. You're everybody.

Don't smile, though. Not now, not this deep into it.

You knew better than to come out tonight, of course, in a city you know only by name, a convention destination you hadn't even planned on, but doing what you know you shouldn't, it makes your chest swell with satisfaction, too.

It's not impulse overriding fear—you're not that base—it's commitment asserting itself, it's recognizing your own hesitation as timidity, which would be even more base to submit to.

Walking back into the din and rush of the bar, nobody can see the grin that almost ghosts the corners of your mouth up.

You track her in the mirror as she tracks your progress back to your seat, and you're tempted to drop a nod her way, just to see how she curls her lips, or if she doesn't, but then her eyes do a thing you weren't expecting: they give an irritated flick to the opposite corner, by the fire door.

Seriously?

No.

You've got to look, though.

Forty-eight seconds later (count them out on your cocktail napkin), you turn to the sound of a fan belt screeching in the street like a dying bird, and take in that dark corner. That corner she didn't mean to give away.

A man. Just as nondescript as you.

His drink is watery, old.

You twist your seat back around, your eyes hot with possibility: her plan, then, it's—it's *not* to take him back to his place, slip him a pill, do a little late-night shopping. Pretend she's the lady of the house for a few hours. Watch his chest rise and fall, a cloth napkin draped across his face so she won't have to keep seeing him. Maybe stage a photo opportunity or two.

This is something else.

And—you see it, and now that you do, how did you miss it? The bridge of her nose, her profile in the mirror. She's like a Picasso painting, has probably been told all her life that she has a classic grace. Which is another way of saying that the bridge of her nose, it's like the spinal crest you've seen on dinosaurs, in artists' recreations: instead of forming a saddle, it's a straight line up to the forehead, a clean ridge of flesh. A Roman nose, one that fills out the hollow spaces of a Centurion helmet.

And the man in the corner, covering the exit, he has it as well. Meaning that when he looks back at you, it's straight-on, as his inner peripheral vision is next to nothing.

Brother and sister? Either that or—either that or it's happening. They're coming for you, they're slinking into every background, are going to replace the crowd around you one by one, until you're surrounded.

Because they know. They're leaking in from, from—

No.

It makes your heart slap the inside of your chest, makes your throat dry, but no.

And don't let it show. Never let it show.

They're just a couple of freaks. A pair of coincidences who maybe know each other in some way. If you study hard enough, you can probably find two different people in the bar with lips that match, with earlobes from the same genetic strain, with the same college on their diplomas.

Cycle down, cycle down.

Curl back over your drink as if it's why you're here, and, two seats down, your skinny man, your stick man, your man with the nicotine-stained fingers and the raspy breath, let him rattle the leftover ice from his scotch into his mouth, crunch it harshly enough between his teeth that you have to cringe, try to swallow that sound away.

If you weren't already committed to him, then that would have decided it for you, yes.

Certain people, they need your services. They're asking for them.

Who are you to deny them?

As for this 'Stick Man,' it's a temporary name, of course. Like always. But you have to call him something. And it does fit. Unlike his billowy jacket. Unlike what looks like his father's pants, pilfered from another decade. His hands always opening and closing, as if he's used to wearing thick gloves, is luxuriating in the tactile sensations of this world. It's his eyes that initially got your attention, though. How they're hollowed out with fear, like he saw himself in the three-way mirror at some department store, fled directly here to drown his sorrow.

Don't smile.

This Stick Man, though—do it right, you could fold him into a canvas bag, probably. Sling him over your shoulder. Go gallivanting through the wet streets, his large jacket over your own.

Then take him back to your room, dig in, see if it's pharmaceuticals or marathons eating all his fat for him.

It's not that you're jealous—of his emaciation?—it's just that you need to know, that you won't be able to sleep until you do.

And he wants to tell you. He really really does, with every last fiber of his being. He wouldn't be here like this otherwise.

His eventual answer—you know this just as surely as you know the sun will smolder up in the morning—what he'll tell you in not so many words after all the running and screaming, the praying and pleading, it won't be true or false, it won't be multiple choice. It'll be the very distinct sound of a high-temper blade scraping up along the long bone of his thigh, his lips and tongue already macerated, his lone eye roving to your briefcase, open on the hotel bed.

What dark instruments glitter up from that cavity?

None.

The instrument, it's you.

Now you can smile.

If you follow him back to the bathroom, where you know there's an exit door, then do that, and do it properly. If not, then why are you even here?

Good. You made it.

Your room for this is 1807, closest to the stairs. But this is the hotel *across* the street from the one with your name in the system.

You're not stupid, after all.

Card keys—you can't bluff them across the registration desk like you can in the movies, but in any bar on any given night there will be purses everywhere, and it's easy to tell who won't be returning to their own room. Just watch for the woman laughing the hardest. How her eyes aren't as open as her mouth.

The world was made for people like you.

As for Stick Man, by the time he comes to you've already used the heating element from the taken-apart hairdryer to try to melt his lips together, then experimented with the thinner skin of his left eyelid.

"You should . . . you should let me be," he manages to say, his one good eye settling on you.

Say "Be what?" down to him with just a normal, uninterested voice, like you're working the register of this particular late-night grocery store. Like he's just another customer to scan past. Into the afterlife.

He laughs about it as best he can, even going so far as to close his eye, let his head fall back onto the two pillows you've provided.

You're not a monster, after all.

Still, his hands are tied, his feet are tied. He's been stripped, and waxed. And there was the incident with the hair dryer, of course, which, if you had to admit it, you kind of do regret, yes.

Lean back on the particle-board dresser, feel it insubstantial under you. This whole world is made of cardboard.

"What are they saying to you?" Stick Man asks, his eyes still closed.

Bite your cheeks in. Don't take this bait. This insult.

Tell him you're not one of those kind. That you're not like that. Except say it by not saying anything.

"Not talking about the, the *mommy* voices in your head . . ." he goes on, smiling to himself about it then just staring up at the ceiling. In defeat, yes, but not the kind you want. This defeat, it's more like he's just tried explaining calculus to a second-grader.

There's no way here in 1807 to test, but he has to be years-deep into some narcotic. There's no other explanation for his dissociation. No other explanation for his blunt tongue, feeling out the new contours of what's left of his lips. Not testing for pain, you don't think, but simply curious at this new development.

Drugs are what's starved him down. He's no runner.

"Thank you," he says then, rolling his head to settle you in his eye, "my, my angel of involuntary surgery, my, my—"

Lower your face-shield before he can finish, so you don't have to hear.

Words are worms, can live in your head for years if you let them in.

So, don't.

Just lean over him, get to work.

In the morning you have to deliver a talk on heating systems for high-traffic first-floor operations like banks and daycares. Your presentation is waiting on your laptop. All the red arrows on the slides, they glow, they pulse with life, they take the audience's eye deeper into the heat, to the core, and the font you've chosen has no shading, is simply precise, direct, though you had to adjust the contrast a bit to work with the unforgiving background, keep the edges from smearing.

At the end of your fifty minutes there will be the usual round of polite applause, the obligatory question or two, and then you'll retire to your room for the day to clean under your fingernails, perhaps turn the hotel's thermostat all the way down and then call the front desk, complain about it. Just to get a warm body knocking on your door, interacting with you, confirming that, yes, you're still here. And so is everybody else.

The days after nights like these, you need that confirmation again and again, until the feelings settle and you focus, finally take your first real breath.

Sawing through Stick Man's gummy breastbone, the leading point of your saw dulled so as not to puncture the heart sac, you walk your talk through the paces. Mentally click through the slides, leaving the proper pause after each one resolves, so the audience can study its breadth and depth before you pull them into the unwavering lope of your voice.

Under your blade, Stick Man writhes and screams as he has to, but the pillowcase muffles the most of it, and the rest, what spills past, is just what you expect to hear next door in any hotel.

Crack the chest open, not pulling your face away from the heat that fogs your face-shield, and then fix one of the hotel's complimentary pens there, to keep it open. So you can watch the heart glisten down, give up beat by beat. It's not the best part, not your favorite by far, but you feel a certain obligation to witness it, don't you?

As for the teeth, they come out as easy as you'd expect of an addict, some of them wired together in the most antique way—street dentistry?—and the muscles of Stick Man's thigh aren't just starved down, they're limpid, atrophied, sucked dry. His body mass index, it's got to be in the single digits, if not bottomed out completely. It's a surprise his organs haven't stopped working yet.

What are they saying to you?

Click: next slide.

Flay the opaque sheath of connective tissue away from Stick Man's femur now, scraping the bone delicately, lingering on the feel of that sound through the handle of your knife, then let the blade continue up over the scream-tight skin of the lower abdomen.

The warmth of his gut rises up, caresses your hand, leaches through your rubber apron as you stare into his blooming pupil, and, for the first time since you started this journey four years ago, the man under your blade's body shudders with laughter, with gratitude.

Laugh with him, amplify it back at him to allay your own hesitations, but—your hand, the one that just slit his stomach open.

That's not just body heat rising up your wrist, wisping up your sleeve. There's actual steam.

Step away, retreat to the bathroom, come back better though it's hard to be absolutely sure how long you were gone.

Long enough, it looks like: Stick Man's dead, the hotel pen leaking blue ink down onto the heart, the ink tracing the veins out for some reason. Like it knows something. Had always known.

And—if a life bleeds out on a dirty mattress and nobody's there to witness it, did it really even happen?

Probably.

There's the mess, now, anyway.

Shake your head in disappointment, in disgust, then step to the bed and pull at the sides of his abdomen hard enough that the skin tears up to the sternum, joins that incision, so that his whole torso is opening, a chrysalis almost, on its own biologic timer.

Your initial idea, vague but promising—this from a drunk joke Stick Man was trying to tell in the bar, the punch line of which required his whole body—was to massage a section of the intestine until it became elastic enough to stretch over his face like a rubber mask. Just, one with a trunk, twisting down into his own gut.

It had been an elephant joke, yes.

As preparation, you even pocketed a stapler from the desk downstairs, in case the mask slipped.

Now, though.

This is getting away from you. It can never get away from you.

Count to three, count to three again, and reach into Stick Man's gut, come up with his large intestine, just to see what the source of this heat could even be. Can gut bacteria be exothermic? If he'd been muling drugs and a condom broke, would that produce heat? Is he a bomb, did he have something radioactive implanted in his abdomen?

None of the above.

Lift his slick intestine up. Palpate the hard clumps consti-pated in there, evenly spaced like you can find in a large game animal if you take it unaware, before it can void. But.

This is *too* hard. Too regular. The lumps far too large.

You cough in spite of yourself, reach your other hand out, and deliver up into the light a segment of large intestine with a string of petrified tangerines in it. It looks for all the world like peas in a pod, or—no. You *know* what it looks like.

It makes your skin cold.

Used to, before everything, your mother would take you and your brother to the park in town. And there were those trees there with the leathery seedpods, curled back on themselves like half moons. You and your brother would scream, walking over them on the concrete. The way they crunched. And then you'd always try to steal some away home. And your mother would have to pull over for you to throw them away, and, pulling away, did you always sneak looks back? Because maybe something was already growing there. Maybe something would be. Maybe if you looked hard enough, you could see those first delicate tendrils, reaching out for the soil.

This is what Stick Man's large intestines remind you of.

Your brother on the merry-go-round, his head slung back in joy, your mother across all the wood chips, reading her magazine like there's going to be a test.

What might grow from this pod, though?

Your jaw moves, opening your mouth two times, three times. In the most primal joy you've ever lucked onto. No words, no sounds, just a pleasure at the very center of your being, radiating out to your fingernails so you have to snap over and over to keep it in.

You snip the intestine at both ends, tie them off with thin strips of bed sheet, and, because you know this is larceny of the highest order, that this is plundering the past, smuggling it into the present, you clean yourself up in the bathroom, doing a poor job of it but there's no time, there's no time.

After policing the room a second time, kissing Stick Man on

the forehead in thanks then wiping those lip prints away, tuck this section of intestine up your sleeve as best you can, count to three before stepping out the door, into the hall that opens back onto the world, then go back, hang the DO NOT DISTURB sign on the knob.

If you take the stairs, now, then there's the chance a seed will slip out your sleeve on the long way down, crack open on a step, so don't do that. Please, you have to save them, you have to keep them safe. Instead take the elevator, your reflection in all four walls around you, taunting you.

Don't listen to them.

You've got what matters.

Click: next slide.

Thirty-two sales engineers show up for the nine o'clock panel. Bleary-eyed, balancing coffee before them, their name badges askew, pockets lined with business cards.

As there was no eight o'clock panel, show up twenty minutes early, to double-check connectivity, make sure the projector's bulb heats up, and—this is important—re-space the chairs throughout the room, giving the attendees slightly more leg space. As if they're flying business class for this, not coach.

It's the kind of thing that can make a presentation a more pleasant memory, and that kind of unacknowledged comfort tends to associate itself over time with the content of the presentation itself, which can then lead to favoring one process or product over another. Selling air conditioners and heating units, you need every advantage.

There was a time in your life when you would have seen such preparation as insurance, as fallback, as hedging against your own abilities—as gambling against yourself, expecting to fail. But then you realized the obvious: everybody sitting out there, they were all marionettes. That just because you knew where their strings were, and how to manipulate them, that should in no way reflect poorly on you.

Now greet them with an aside—start twice, pretending to ask for their attention rather than owning it whenever you want—an aside not about air circulation at all, but about how you're lobbying for Vegas next year. And for no panels before lunch. Then toast them with the public coffee you've yet to drink from.

A few stray claps and a chuckle or two are your cue to casually stab a finger down to the keyboard of your laptop, the lights dimming, and now you're rolling, reciting, illustrating the slides with your words, using your laser pointer to underline, to circle, your voice a metronome, an antique pocket watch swaying back and forth, back and forth.

If you started at the back of the room and went one by one, you could cut all these people's necks open, moving up row by row, speaking the whole while, clicking the slides with the remote held between your teeth. Just plant your left hand on their clammy foreheads, slip the blade across their tracheas then pull it across two more inches, for their weak spouts of blood.

But not today.

Click, click, bank, daycare, statistic, time of day, draw a red line from this door to that counter, then—*what?*

Polite laughter from the front row.

A giant moth is fluttering against the screen. Trained on an older generation of projector, your hand reaches down, brushes at your laptop screen.

And now there's two moths in high definition.

Pocket your laser so they won't see your hand, balled into a fist.

Is it even the right season for moths? Shouldn't they still be pupating in dark corners, under moldy leaves?

You step into the light, try to sweep the two moths away from the hot glass in front of the projector's bulb.

Instead of sweeping, the moths smear, the blood black and lumpy, darkening the room even more.

Study the back of your hand. Turn it over to check the palm.

Working from the old wives' tale that it would be poison, you have of course collected the silt-fine dust from the backs of scores of moths, smeared them on the pink, fragile gumlines of people tied to chairs.

But you'd let those moths go, too, if not the people. Meaning they should have no grievance against you. The moths. They should have no call to interrupt your presentation like this. They've got no stake, no commission on the line.

Still.

One lands on the hand you're studying, its delicate proboscis tasting the microchasm between your cuticle and fingernail.

Another lands on your tie.

You pinch it away by the wing, fully intending to let it flutter away, but, like the others, it's soft, not formed properly yet. You have to flick it away. Onto the forehead of a pantsuited woman in the front row, who reels back, clawing at her face.

Reach for her as if to help, to apologize, but don't touch.

There's blood on your hands, see.

And then, behind you—turn, look, take it in, you'll never see this again—the projector screen, it's crawling with moths. It's a black and white science fiction movie from the fifties. It's the apocalypse.

Worse—no no no: your briefcase. It's coated with wings, now. The moths' hundreds of feelers surely dialing the brass spinners of the combination lock, trying to luck onto what used to be your brother's birthday. A series of numbers your mom probably can't even remember without having to concentrate.

But these moths, they know.

Inside that briefcase, because you couldn't bear to leave it up in your room for the cleaning woman to scream over, is the lumpy section of Stick Man's large intestine, rubbed with complimentary lotion to keep it from cracking.

What you have now, it's a dilemma, isn't it?

Think of it as a chance to prove yourself, though. That's all everything is.

Go through it blow by blow.

You can rescue the woman in the front row from her own hysterics, and in the process take a sort of responsibility for this infestation, when everybody knows it can't possibly be your fault.

Score one for the good guys.

But then too you can neatly unplug the projector and laptop and lock the door, dispose of the witnesses. It's something you've always wondered about anyway. What it might be like to get dropped into a barrel of sheep, then turn the lights off so that all that's left for a flash would be your smile.

Then there'd be the mess, though. The explanations. Being the sole survivor. Probably having to suffer some self-inflicted nearly-mortal wound you'd then have to recover from for months, limiting your travels.

You could do it, of course, and do it well—like you always say: sacrifices—but, in some jam-up years down the road, if the authorities scrolled back to this, then that'd be a strike against *you*, wouldn't it? At a time when you might need no strikes at all.

Another option is just reaching for that briefcase, scores of tiny bodies wriggling between your palm and the leather handle. And then not wriggling.

Simplest is always best, isn't it?

But not yet.

First, close your laptop, wincing from the wet resistance that almost keeps it from clicking all the way shut.

Next, standing in the light so that your face is underlit like this is a scary story told at a campfire, say it, the only thing that can work as an exit line: "They don't have moths in Vegas, do they?"

Now, now collect your laptop, tuck it under your arm, and, working calmly, as if you'd really rather leave it here in the disaster, wipe the moths from your briefcase handle and pull it up, shake it once, dislodging what you can of this morning's disaster.

Some of the moths will fall to the low-rise institutional carpet, but the bulk of them will find their wings, flutter up into the projector's light.

In that mild panic that's soon to dissolve to embarrassed laughter—they're just *moths*—slip out. Keep going, your pace unhurried, your lips pleasant.

Your eyes, though.

Some things even you can't help.

Because the cleaning lady's still in your room, judging you, using scotch tape to capture any hairs you've left, her apron lined with evidence baggies—all cleaning staff is like this—retreat to the parking garage. Take the stairwell up into the sky.

The moths don't follow.

If they found you by scent, then there's too much out here. Or maybe their eyes aren't ready for the sun.

Check your briefcase now, yes.

Spin to that magic date, pop it open in your lap.

They're still there. Just the same, the internal fabric seams of the briefcase caulked with children's glue—all they had at the store down the way. And these eggs, these seeds, they're glistening and regular in their sausage sheath. Dab at a fleck of the lotion. Caress it in deeper. Watch it disappear under your finger, a missive from you to them: it's okay, it's okay.

Take your heartbeat down, now. Let yourself rest, go cold at the extremities, calm at the center. Picture the cleaning lady's head in the paper bag of her vacuum cleaner, looking out through the zipped-open birthing slot. Hide the rest of her in the dresser drawers. Fold her between the pages of the directory, alphabetized in a way the next cleaning lady will recognize. Force her through the grate of the heater. Call her kids so they can hear her not say anything anymore ever again. Call Thomas so he can whisper to her.

Your brother, yes.

He would know what to say to her, wouldn't he?

It's because of where he lives now.

There's a different language, there. You know there has to be. One that goes directly to the spine. To the tight muscles at the base of the jaw. To the heart that's deeper than your real heart.

Thomas.

It's okay, nobody's up here, and you've already rolled the briefcase's lock to random numbers, so, if you die right here and now, of happiness, nobody will know what you were thinking when it happened.

What are they saying to you? Stick Man had asked.

Fuck him.

He didn't know anything, didn't know that you always tried to protect him, Thomas. Not because of blood, but because people said you looked alike. But you knew better, were already studying him then. How he only had a few of your features, like he got the leftovers in your mom's stomach, wasn't as prime a specimen. Or, like you'd taken all the good, didn't know anybody else was coming through. So, you were always making it up to him, day by day. Apologizing that he didn't come out right. As right as you did, anyway. As pure.

It was the least you could do.

But you had to sleep at some point, didn't you?

Back then you did, anyway.

And that was when it happened.

He didn't run away because he was petulant or ill-behaved or a miscreant, though, like your mom would say to the police later. It wasn't even the right park. Didn't they know anything? Weren't they the *police*?

No, the reason he ran away, it had to do with the seed pod you'd finally managed to sneak home. She found it under Thomas's pillow, the most obvious place, but he was just a kid, too. Had probably meant it as some sort of trade for the Tooth Fairy. Or left it there just so he could sneak touches up to it all night. Whisper secrets to it. Make promises. Lick it clean when nobody was looking.

But she found it like she always did, like she could detect each flake of skin in the house, each mote of dust, each bad thought, and she marched the two of you out front to dispose of it in the trash can, to lecture you about cleanliness and foreign bodies and little stealers, each of you in your underwear.

And you didn't punch him for sneaking your pod from your secret box in the closet. But you might have broken your own rules and pinched him as if he were your equal, as if he had the faculties to control himself, wasn't just falling victim to being put together from pieces that hadn't been good enough for you.

And he didn't tell on you for the pinching, that was the thing. He loved you too much to get you in trouble. Or, he knew he deserved it, was probably pinching himself under the covers as well.

What he did to make up for it, then, it probably made perfect sense in his head. To his way of thinking. After lights out eyes

Stephen Graham Jones

shut, he creaked his way to the front door, let himself out into the night, to get you another seed pod. He left to somehow walk all those miles to the park, come back with an impossible prize.

And that's where they found his light blue windbreaker with the darker blue tiger stripes on the side like ribs: at the top of the slide at the park. The wrong park. The one just down the street, not all the way across town.

How old he was, he probably didn't even understand that there was more than one park in the world.

The jacket was hanging on the tallest pole, a flag. Up where Thomas couldn't have even reached, and why would he have taken his jacket off in the first place? To sit on it to make the slide faster, maybe, or to keep the dew from his jeans. But not because he was hot. It never broke fifty degrees that night.

No, that jacket, there. They were supposed to find it.

This language, these signs, they already came so naturally to you, didn't they? You knew the fundaments of this life already. The real way of speaking. The only way that matters.

What you didn't tell the police was that the jacket was supposed to make it look like Thomas had climbed the ladder in the dark, sat down to ride through that brief tunnel, then never made it out the other side. Like the night had just gulped once, swallowed him whole.

Which is exactly what it did.

Which was so much better than knowing, than finding, than seeing pictures. Because then you got to imagine. In high detail. Every time you closed your eyes. A thousand sordid lives for Thom to live out. To be pushed headfirst through, screaming the whole while. But the more variations you could think of, then the longer he was alive, right? And being alive's better. Being alive's the best.

It wasn't easy, thinking of all that all the time, but it's not like your mom was going to do it.

And it's all been worth it, too. Now—after all this time, you've finally cut deep enough into the world that it had to give up one of its secrets. One of its most dear secrets.

Thank you.

By the time you cue into the footsteps approaching behind you, the footsteps that don't care if you hear them, the footsteps that don't hesitate, that don't even know hesitation, your hands are of course slick with your own saliva. Because you didn't have any more hotel lotion to rub into Stick Man's intestines.

Just close the briefcase like you're filing a paper, though.

Don't wipe your hands on the concrete, because that'll leave a dark smear.

And, most important, don't run, never run, running is a temporary solution, but don't come up fast either, leading with the edge of your briefcase. Though you could. You definitely could. And who would know.

The footsteps scrape to a stop behind you. Waiting.

Smile to yourself because they don't know anything.

The shadows falling to either side of you are one blocky male, one tall female. Man, woman, and, between, your own sitting shadow, like a child.

Not for long, though.

Look to your right sharply, as if to the sound of a door closing, a car only your keen senses can detect, but keep your eyes on the silhouette those two faces can't help but cut, what with the sun still low, coming in at a harsh angle.

Like you were dreading, two classical profiles look to their right with you to that make-believe sound. Two Roman Centurions, on guard.

And you, you're just a businessman, of course, a representative for your company, up for some fresh air, some sun, some distance from this debacle of a presentation you just tried to lead. Some space to mourn all the sales you just lost, all the commission you were counting on.

And your hands, they're almost dry, now. Just tacky.

Don't smell them. Maybe just a little, to be sure.

The man coughs into his hand, announcing himself like a butler. The woman's still looking to the right. As if seeing something there after all.

Or else she's trying to get you to look that way again as well.

"Shit, I forgot to turn the projector off—" you say with a startled grin, standing and facing them in one casual, non-threatening move.

They just stare down at you.

You're tall, but they have maybe four inches on you—even the woman, as if the only real difference between the two of them is their sex. If that. Their haircuts, anyway. Their clothes.

And there's that direct way they have of settling you in their line of sight, their eyes forever separate from each other. Like they're grazers.

Making you what in relation to them, right?

Don't grin. Keep it inside. Open and close your hand in anticipation of a possible meet and greet. If your palm sticks to them, then your face will probably stick in their heads as well. And you can't have that.

But there are ways, of course. To scoop memories out. And a lot else besides. Right now, though, your 'projector' is still hanging in the air, the slowest butterfly. But still, they're waiting.

"You are from the front desk, aren't you?" you say, switching the briefcase to your other hand.

The woman smiles a tolerant smile here.

"You mean you're—you're not with the hotel?" you say. "I'm sorry, I just . . . Downstairs, my meeting room, it was—hardly interesting to you, I'm sure."

With that, nod once, start to slide by.

Except the man has his long fingers to your bicep, now.

"Scotch, right?" the woman says.

It's what you were drinking last night. What you still haven't made up for properly.

And the man's fingers, even through the sleeve of your suit jacket, they're cold, they're marble.

"Don't listen to them," the man says to you then, his voice safe like a preacher's. "You can't listen to them."

"I think you've got me . . ." you say, speaking slow to show your honest confusion, feeling your way through the word. Moving around the tall man's hard fingers one by one. Getting the sun behind you.

"It's too late," the woman says to the man, lowering her face to look into your eyes as if you're a specimen. As if she wants to look through, into your head.

Do they even blink?

"Scotch," you repeat, turning your face away from her penetrating gaze. From the individual fibers of her iris, which were—but they couldn't have been—in motion. Crawling.

What you want to do here, it's run for the edge of the parking garage, that thick half wall before all that open space, and dive out, wait for a pillow of moth bodies to cushion itself under you, take you with them.

At least until you catch a moth fluttering from the man's crisp sleeve.

He sees you take note of this. Cups his other hand over his offending wrist. A groomsman, just waiting for this ceremony to complete itself.

You too.

If you scratch at his face now, to see if there's blood under there or dusty wings, then that'll leave the woman behind you, where she could potentially grab the briefcase, run off with Thomas. Or just drop him. Or raise him as her own, but with a different name, which would be the most sincere type of violence you can even begin to imagine.

So.

What real choice do you have, right?

It's ugly, but let yourself be led between them and only look back once, as the three of you are ducking into the fetid stairwell, its steps tacky like your hands. You know from the walk up, how it was like the stairs were soft, were a cushion, were something you could step into up to your knee if you weren't careful.

But you made it to the top. You always do.

And it's not over yet, this ceremony.

Two buildings over there's a piece of cloth tied to an antenna, fluttering once in the wind then lying slack. Part of you must have noticed it early, lodged it in your head for precisely this opportunity.

What you need to do, now, it's watch that flag long enough that it keeps you from taking the next step down, the step that will jack the half wall up between you and it. Long enough that the man will look back to it as well, trying to parse his way through that distant language. Long enough that the woman will catch his urgency and step back up herself, to look over the wall, see this artifact for herself.

While they're distracted, and while they're at ease, are just two of three reasonable people heading downstairs for the bar, for reasonable conversation, whip your belt from its loops, wrap it around the man's neck and keep him between you and the woman.

His legs, kicking and spasming, will help. It's what you

imagine strangling a stork might be like. When his hands claw up, too, it's not at his own neck, but back farther, for you, like he doesn't understand what's happening here.

Some people are born to die.

After he's gone, let him drop, toss her the guilty belt so she has to flinch her left arm up for it.

With her side exposed like that, come up with the corner of the briefcase, feel her ribs crunch into her right lung, then follow her down, open her face on the metal-lipped corner of the concrete stair, then open it some more, then push with your knee to be sure, her scream, if she could scream, directed straight into the concrete.

It's quiet now, isn't it? Except for your breathing. But you can control that.

Scan the roof for the cameras you already know aren't there—breathe, breathe—and then, for the benefit of anybody watching from the building across the street, their view obscured by the half wall, keep talking to this man and this woman as you switchback down the stairwell, ready to turn on a dime if footsteps are coming up to meet you.

When they do, let them pass you on what looks to them like your way up, become just another businessman ducked down to his cellphone.

It's a couple, good.

Let them find the bodies, ring the alarm.

By then you're across the skywalk, are moving briskly through the lobby, smiling your way into a handshake with a lanky man from the second row of your presentation. Leave him with a business card from your left pocket, which is where you put cards you've *collected*, then offer to pick up the dry-cleaning on his tie, which he'll of course wave away, because that obligates him.

Keep your real name in your right pocket, though.

Then, after taking the elevator up, take it back down, insist on a different room on a different floor.

If you elect to sit in your room and wait for the sirens, watch the scene unfold on the local news, then you might want to order lunch before the rush. Something vegetarian, say, and tip well, salute the kid back down the hall, into the rest of his life.

But you are who you are, of course.

Instead of ordering in, go over the cleaned room with your clear tape, to see what traps and indicators this other cleaning lady's left, then pack a towel behind the heating grate, turn the shower on for sound and open your briefcase on the second bed, holding your breath until the lock pops.

All six of them are there, leathery and brown in their intestinal pod, but one of them is crowning, is nudging its way from a newly ruptured end. Ruptured from the impact, you know. From her. From *them*.

It'll make your shoulders shake, your throat catch, your mouth open and close again.

Turn off the lights.

Ride it out.

Your dreams are the usual dreams.

Don't worry about them.

Walk naked to the curtains pulled across your wide wide window.

Slide those curtains open and then, when they're still not open, look to the octagonal stick in your hand, to make sure it's actually connected to the rail. Then wipe at the dark glass.

It squeaks, is cold.

A lazy triangle of light opens up under your palm.

Moths.

And, because this is the outside, butterflies as well. Probably bats circling the hotel, waiting for the feast.

Don't call the front desk to tell them. Or, do, but then don't say anything. See if they can hear those legs out there, clinging to the glass.

They can't.

Turn on the news. Promise to remember to remind yourself to eat something.

It's six o'clock already, somehow.

You're losing time. It's a bad sign.

Since the bar last night, when you look back, it's all a smear. With lumps in it. Six of them.

It's not supposed to be funny.

And . . . is this how it happens? Are these the last hours before you betray yourself, before you let them come for you? Before you start decaying on the national news?

No.

It's just a temporary weakness. An understandable hiccup in the usual procession.

It's not every day you find your baby brother sleeping inside another man.

Because you slept through the sirens from the parking garage, wait for those two distinct faces to show up on the news. Well, wait for them to show up if their Roman-nosed family has been notified.

Smile. You're alone, nobody can see.

Click to the other station when this one's just weather, traffic, elections, human interest.

Yes. Two bodies found in the parking garage of a prominent hotel. The usual slurry of emergency vehicles and non-statements. A man, a woman, and, because the authorities need help identifying, sketches of their faces, as photographs would of course offend all the dinner eaters out there.

The man has dark hair, is mid-twenties, and his fiancé, blonde as wheat, she wouldn't even go five-ten in heels.

Lean forward, try to click deeper, make their faces hold on the screen. Chase them to the other news.

No.

This—this is the couple that went up to *find* the bodies, they've got it all wrong.

Turn the thermostat up as high as it will go. Take the towel from the heating grate and leave the grate off, stand there in the blast of warm air. But this shivering, it's not from the cold, is it? And it's not from hunger.

Even if—even if that couple *did* somehow meet their end up there, then still, *still*, that would mean four bodies, wouldn't it?

Can they not do math in this town?

Step into your pants, cinch your belt tighter than you need it to be. The shower's still on, has been. Turn it off, apologize out loud for your forgetfulness. Promise not to let it happen again.

Next, your shirt, your tie, your business face, your hand to the silver knob when there's a scrape on the door.

No breathing now. Just listening.

Again, the scrape.

Place your fingertips to either side of the peephole and lean forward, peer through even though this has to be a trap of some kind, there has to be a police spike on the end of a battering ram, a spike ready to come through the door for your sternum, a spike to nick your spinal cord on its way past, its lethal tip undamaged by all the damage it's caused, is causing.

You can't *not* look, though.

It's another eyeball.

Don't jerk back—flinching is for the weak. Flinching is for whoever's there, trying to look through.

The bellboy? Did he see you salute, take some sort of adolescent umbrage? The cleaning lady, to see if you're asleep yet, if she can creep in? The lanky man from the presentation? Did he know that wasn't your business card, that wasn't your name?

Think about his nose. Was he one of them?

No. And there's no *them* at all. There's just the news, screwing up. Unless—did she *want* you to hit her with the briefcase? Could she judge its weight, its contents, by how deep that rounded-brass corner went into her side? Or was it you she was trying to figure out?

No. No no no.

And the iris in the peephole, it's just normal, striated brown, the pupil drawn down to a point.

And then it jerks away, looks down towards the elevator, that side of his face destroyed—no eye, no lips, no teeth. Anymore.

Stick Man, in all his glory.

Naked, waxed, cracked open. Standing there for all the world to see. Chewing lazily on the pen that colored his heart. Chewing with his gums.

Swallow whatever's risen in your throat, blink long, then look again.

Nothing. Just your breathing. Maybe the brass rollers on your briefcase's lock somewhere behind you. They're creaking. They know what date they want.

If you look through the peephole a third time, here, and see only a different room service boy pushing his cart past, his left hand already shaped like a twenty-percent tip, then rest easy.

If you look through and just see an empty hall, though, well.

Keep looking.

Try not to flinch when the hand cups your shoulder. Pretend you haven't been waiting for it your whole life.

The last thing you remember is the slide.

No. Stupid stupid stupid.

The last thing you remember, it's that different room-service boy in the hall. How, the peephole approaching your face at an accelerated rate, your head whipping on your neck, that hand driving you forward, how what you thought was that kid, he would never know his own ball-and-socket joint, the one that lets him lean forward like that, push his cart. Walk.

That he'd never know unless someone with patience took the time to show him.

And then your face exploded into the wood of the door, and now you're staring up at the ceiling.

Naked, check.

Waxed, yes.

Tied at all four points.

The heating register at the top of the wall blowing for all its worth, the room swampy, a jungle.

"Call me Jack if you want," a voice says from the window.

If you crane your head forward, you can just tease a form out from the shadow of the curtain.

"Thomas?" you say, hopefully.

"Jack," the man corrects, his words lispy and wrong. "You are a man of the twentieth century, are you not? My child, in a way. More ways than one, really."

When he turns to face you, to give you his face, he's Stick Man.

Shudder now.

This is the other end.

You always pictured a slight slit opening up in some forgotten corner, dark fingers pushing through to tear that rip wider, allow your punishment to come surging through, body after body, shadows to embrace you, to rub against you, to whisper into your neck exactly what you've always wanted to hear, which would be the end of you: *We know who you are. We've come to watch. We want to be like you. We're here forever.*

Not interdimensional homicide detectives or unborn children from the future, come back to avenge who should have been their parents, but faceless forms dripping with adoration, watching your every facial tic, so they can mimic, your expressions rippling through all of them like a virus until they crawl inside your mouth, swim in your body, their eyes looking up at you from your own palms until you have to make fists, run and run and run, never stop, your state of panic permanent, no solitude anymore, no death, just a fullness inside, suffocating you.

Except that's not it at all.

What you're getting, what you've got, it's your most recent victim, risen to practice on you what he learned from you.

The long muscle close to your femur twitches once.

"Jack," you say, stalling even though these attempts to dilate the moment, delay the inevitable, they're always so laughable. So obvious.

Still.

Stick Man nods, steps forward. Angles his mangled head over to better study your naked form.

"As in Whitechapel," he says, air hissing through where his teeth once were, then he looks towards the moth-dark window.

Jack the Ripper.

Shake your head in disgust.

Does it even count, if the person who finally eviscerates you, if he's off his rocker, living in some running delusion?

Or, if he's not even real.

"They always find you," he says, placing his bloody palm to the glass of the window, the night darkening there, the moths converging. "Them, I mean," he says, and looks down to the second bed.

To Thomas.

Stick Man grins when you kick and pull against your restraints. Useless.

"What are they saying to you?" he says, moving his hand across the glass slowly, amused by the moths' simplicity, it seems. Like dragging shapes in the sand.

"That you were just holding them," you say. "For me."

Stick Man nods like that's about right.

"I was born during your civil war," he says, boredom in his voice now. "Born with a surgeon's hands, of course. But that— forget it. They make you last, though, the . . . what are you calling them, the eggs? 'Thomas?' I'm guessing that's somebody you used to—"

Tell him that they're not eggs.

"Not eggs?" he says, a bloody approximation of a smile trying to form on his ruined face.

Seeds. But don't say it out loud.

Buck and kick and scream when he goes to the briefcase, though, and, instead of dialing back to the past, he just slams it against the corner of the short bureau.

And again, the contents finally clunking down to the floor.

He looks down to them, counting with his eyes and fingers.

"There were seven when I found them in that whore," he says, and watches for your reaction. "They were whispering in my head for two days before I found her."

"They're just—"

"Shut up! We don't have long, here. They can't be outside the body too long. They start to, well. You know. Hatch."

Now he's lowering himself for one, bringing it up on his fingertips. "Who are you?" he says to it, then cups it with both hands, breathes down onto it and closes his one eye.

"The same year I . . . made my discovery, I, well. You know this, of course. I wanted to see what would happen. The keepers showed me how to get them inside, to carry—it was *surgery*— but you can shit one out if you really want. If you promise to keep it secret. They don't know that, they think they can only be cut out."

"They?"

Stick Man studies you for a few seconds then shrugs, lobs the seed onto your gut. You hollow your belly, catch it, hold it. He steps into the bathroom, does something loud, comes back with a large shard of mirror.

"Hey!" he says to the window, "I need a moment here, guys," and he scoops up another egg, tosses it into the far corner.

The window darkens there, goes clear where Stick Man was standing before. Where he's standing again.

He looks down and lines the mirror up against whatever he's seeing.

"See?" he says, trying to tilt the mirror for you as well.

"What?" you say, the mirror bloody now at the edges, every- thing in it trembling, but, for a flash, a reflection pulls across its surface.

Two pale people, standing guard on the top of the shorter building across the alley. Their faces looking right into the mirror.

Stick Man waves.

"Hitler," he says, not looking over to you. "He was born nine months after I officially retired. Coincidence?"

He comes back to you for the answer.

When you just stare at him he shrugs, holds the mirror out over like a plate, and drops it.

It shatters over your chest but doesn't cut you.

He ferrets up a sliver of it.

"Surgery," he says, grinning, but first collects all the seeds, stacks them on the bed beside you, and—this speaks well for the hotel's choice in mattress—they don't collapse, they hold their crude pyramid.

Stick Man likes it, looks down to you.

"It's you or nobody," he says, showing his own cracked-open torso. "Somebody used me all up, I mean." Then he laughs to himself, says, "You're about to be part of history, did you know that? These eggs, they're older than the world, man. Passed down from large intestine to large intestine. Lost a hundred times, found a hundred more. I think there were twelve when it all began. That sound about right?"

"Don't," you tell him.

This is the pleading. The begging.

Never the best part.

"You know what, though?" he says then, dropping his shard. "Surgery means recovery, and you've got to book it if you want to stay ahead of them. However, the human body being what it is, there are of course alternate points of entry, if you will."

This time he comes back from the bathroom with this room's new supply of hand lotion.

He stirrups your feet up so your knees are in shoulders, and warms the lotion in his hands before rubbing it into you.

"Say ah," he says, his face right in yours as he forces the tapered but-not-tapered-enough leading nose of the first seed against your wet, unrelaxed rectum.

Hold his eyes as best you can, to show him you can take this.

But still.

Your throat swells, and when you finally scream he puts his mouth right against yours and screams back, *with* you, his breath hot in your own mouth, the dry holes where his teeth were dripping dark fluid from him to you.

And then there's five more.

Stick Man was the wrong name.

More like Oyster Man. Oyster Man and his six smooth children.

This has been the night you gained twelve pounds. And your hands, they know what to do, have been kneading the new lumps in your lower abdomen for hours, it feels like. Working them up, in, deeper. The lotion runny in the room's heat, spilling from its bottle beside you.

How is it not all gone, right?

There are mysteries in the world.

Gone as well are your restraints.

And the moths, though it takes you a while to cue into their absence. To ask yourself why the streetlight's bleeding in.

Will there be gooey footprints in the carpet, though? Knee smears to either side of your hips?

You don't want to know. Because you already know, can read the headlines now: Traveling Salesman Forgets Self, Doesn't Eat, Goes Feral in Room 428, Impregnates Self with Stones of Dubious Origin.

No. Try again.

Person Least Likely to Save the World Saves World, Reverse Ingests the World's Lingering Destruction.

Like any of them could really hatch into another Hitler, another Black Plague. Like man wouldn't have spilled these particular beans centuries ago.

But maybe that's why they find the ones like you, think?

Give a gift like this to the best church deacon you know, and inside of two years he'll have saved the world to death.

No, it takes someone with discipline. Someone who's lived a *life* of discipline, of restraint, of control.

Someone like you.

Now, stand if you can. Wait for your inner ears to catch up, right you against this new weight in your gut, this new center of gravity, this new purpose.

Thomas.

Don't even look out the window. They're not going to be there. You're not that weak.

Instead, watch the blood slip down the insides of your thighs.

Something new every day, right?

The world, it's truly a wonderful place. And, yes, you can fashion a butt plug of sorts from common items scavenged from your everyday typical hotel room.

Which is not what this room is anymore.

You've always promised never to burn your real name, the one on the register downstairs.

But you never expected to find Thomas either. After all these years.

Walk away, now. Don't even bother with clothes. Your suit, rumpled and bloody on the floor, it's a chrysalis, could never contain you again.

If you elect to ball up on the second bed, hugging your treasure, if you choose to let sleep take you—you've earned it—then trust that your dreams this time, they'll be of a slate blue body of water, lapping at a shore.

If, however, you find yourself standing at your peephole again, then know that this is your old instincts rising. Not to camp at the scene. Not to chance luxury. Not to be weak.

You don't need the ocean in your head, you need food.

You're eating for seven, now. You're eating for all of mankind.

Walk naked down the hall, daring the elevator doors to open, and knock on the door six down from yours, and across, and hold your thumb over the peephole lens.

That it's the lanky man from the presentation can only mean that this was meant to be.

His clothes are going to fit perfectly.

Two days later, your affair with room service comes to an end.

It's been scrambled eggs by the plateful, and club sandwiches with double sides of home fries, and chicken and chicken and chicken, cracking the drumstick bones open to lap at the black marrow.

Not beef, as your body rejects that now, but beasts of the air, anyway.

And you haven't turned the lights on even once. And you've tipped well, have been presentable each time that knock comes to the door. And the trays, you walk them down to the elevator bay, so as not to draw attention, and each of those journeys through the light, they're like walking through suspended motor oil, unburned motor oil, and the faces you see, the other hotel guests, they seem trapped in amber, there on display for your amusement.

You could harvest any of them, but only want chicken, for now.

And coleslaw, once you find it on the menu.

Coleslaw with ketchup, and the tap doesn't have enough water, and still, you can already feel the long muscles of your thigh withering.

It's good you're going to have to use one of the backup names, now. It's fitting, for the new person you're becoming.

But now management's calling. Not about the extended stay, but about the ringing phone. The lanky man's wife, having a panic attack from five hundred miles away.

So be it.

Pack his suitcase, tie his understated tie and cinch it up to your throat, rasp your fingers over the stubble on your jaw and study your face in the mirror from every angle.

You killer.

Smile, tap the glass goodbye, and hang the DO NOT DISTURB sign on the brushed aluminum handle before leaving.

At the elevator, a cleaning lady is collecting your mound of dishes.

Pretend they're not yours. That you don't know what she's thinking about you. That you don't know she's sneaking looks at you from under her bangs.

Twelve minutes and forty-seven seconds later, leave most of her in the supply closet, but bury the soles of her feet in the ice machine.

Because there's change in the lanky man's slacks, you might as well get a candy bar for the ride to the lobby, too. Maybe a soda.

While trying to decide which one, a bleary-eyed woman (nod hey to her, that you're no threat, are just on your way out, here) will crack the ice machine open behind you, dig her bucket full in one scoop.

Don't turn around. Never turn around. Just wait for your drink to fall.

In the elevator—brass hand rails but just wood paneling, no mirrors—you can study your hand. Opening, closing. Like a glove you've just pulled on.

It fits.

This is what you've been waiting for your whole life, like a word on the end of your tongue, one you know is there but that you can't quite articulate the shape of, the sound of. This is what you would have been looking for, had you known to look.

But sometimes life finds you, too.

Swallow your grin as the lobby approaches—better unassuming than smug for the walk past Registration—and look away when the door dings open, one floor shy.

It's them.

Him, her.

They step in, assume positions to either side of you, an errant moth trailing in behind them, fluttering dumbly against the roof.

The door swishes shut.

Well.

"You're dead," you say to the two of them.

No response.

It's best that there aren't any mirrors.

Too, there's maybe eighteen seconds before the doors open again, on the crowd of humanity.

"Don't," the woman says.

What she's talking about—you all know it—is the parking garage stairwell. What she's talking about is the elevator doors opening onto the lobby, you stepping out in a borrowed suit, stepping out over the two steaming bodies you've just cracked open, straightening your tie, then walking away.

They wouldn't fight back, you know. It's not in their nature, somehow. It's like a poem you read once, how animals that are born prey, when the shadow falls over them, they just arch their backs into it and close their eyes, bite the backs of their cheeks inward, in pleasure.

"Don't listen to them," the man adds, and you narrow your eyes about this.

Stick Man said it. The man said it before. The woman seconded it.

It must be how you found him all those nights ago, in the bar, telling his extravagant jokes, holding his drink so cavalierly. A fate you sensed, through all that smoke and regret. A destiny lined nose to tail in another man's intestines.

Something only you could have picked up on. Something that was calling to you, and only to you.

This is nothing new.

Switch the lanky man's briefcase to your other hand, now, to both hands, and let it hang in front of you like a rectangular scrotum, and flash that you're the groom, now. That this is the rest of your life.

And that the ceremony, it's almost over.

It's best that there's no mirrors for this ride.

It's best that they can't see your face.

Ask them, "What are you?"

Look over to the man when neither of them answer.

"We're tired," he'll say, and you can see it in his eyes, that he's not lying. The fatigue of ages, it's heavy on him. On both of them.

That this elevator car can even shoulder this weight, man.

Grin a bit, with one side of your mouth.

Tell them you're out.

Now they're both looking at you in that direct, disconcerting way they have.

Heft the briefcase to show what you mean by "out."

The moth flutters down from above your heads, lands near the handle. Near your hand.

Shake the case once so they can hear the heaviness inside.

Look from her to him, from him to her, the elevator dinging all around the three of you now.

He nods, once, and you nod once in return, just businessmen conducting their business, then you lower the case to the floor under the wall of buttons, the doors whispering open before you.

"Guess this is forever," you say to them, to her, and step forward.

The woman's already reaching for the case.

Step past, through, and, on the way out, reach back, tap the button for the top floor.

By the time they get there, they'll have found the rest of the cleaning lady, smeared in with the lanky man's business proposals.

And you, you'll have four minutes on them, maybe five.

For someone like you, yes, that can be forever. Now shake the moth from the back of your hand, walk into it.

Five years is nothing, now.

Stick Man was right: your body, it turns to beef jerky, but beef jerky, it stays on the shelf forever, doesn't it?

You don't know how long you can go on, really. As long as you're carrying, probably. Or until someone like you finds you.

That's been the only fear, and the best lesson.

Before, you were always the wolf, weaving through the big sheep party. Now, though, now you want to keep your head down. Now you have something to protect.

You stay away from the bars, from the usual places.

You keep moving, too. Small town to small town. Because the Centurions, the angels, the keepers, the minders, whatever they are, they've got to be expecting you to follow the old patterns. But the city centers, the anonymous faces, that's not for you anymore.

Or Thomas.

Another good thing about small towns is that the motel rooms aren't clean in the first place.

This world was made for you, yes.

In a town with 'Deer' in the front part of it, not two months after slipping below the radar, dying your hair, injecting your lips, changing your name every week, developing a limp that needed a cane sometimes, when that's when you wanted the clerk's eyes to fall, in Deer Something, Thomas was born again.

You had the sterilized exacto knife hovered above your shaved stomach, were nodding to yourself that this was right, that this was the only way, but then your shoulders hunched around each other and you started gagging.

Something was crawling up your esophagus.

Hundreds of little wet feet scrabbling. Leathery eggshell in your gut, left behind.

On all fours between the wall and the double bed, you tried to scream into the carpet, instead threw up your little brother.

He was segmented, shiny, and shy of the light, humped his way immediately into the dark safety under the bed and stayed there for days, curled in on himself, hissing.

Because you're a good big brother, too, a good father, you of course fed him. Not what you would have expected him to eat— what you could harvest from the kitchens of the farm houses all around, from the stream of cars passing through the gas station across the street—but leaves, and berries, and nuts when you could find them.

Three months later he stood up beside the bed you were sleeping on, tugged at the sheets, a little boy with pale hair and pale eyes and no saliva that you could detect, no scent whatsoever.

You pulled him under with you, kept him warm, made him promises.

His scalp smelled so new.

And then you left, and left the next place, and the place after that, driving slow into the future, both hands on the wheel, and you waited for him to say a word, to speak, to use his vocal apparatus at all.

But maybe that takes longer, when you've come as far as he has. And you could talk for the both of you, anyway. Instruct him on ways to avoid detection, how to harvest, how never to harvest. Who to select, who's worth waiting for, who to let go. Your whole life has been training for this.

You always knew there was a reason, didn't you?

But the city beckons.

Your rationale is that *their* reasoning, it has to be that you've been keeping to the rural parts. So, while they're out there in the hinterlands, letting their moths go again and again—camphor in your pockets was all it took—you can come to where they aren't. It's logical. And, no, they're not herding you. Rather, this is a merry chase, an adventure. No rush at all.

You feed Thomas from the produce section of the health food store, walk hand in hand to the car.

In the slot next to yours is a woman leaned into the passenger seat, arranging groceries. Nobody in the whole wide world watching her. You stand there, appraising her, and finally realize this is a test. That everything's orchestrated, synchronized. That she's waiting to see if you're the same anymore. If you're still you.

Not a test, an invitation.

Come back. Remember us?

Yes.

But walk away.

Buckle Thomas into his seat, pull your door closed and ease out, take random streets through the more and more familiar buildings until dusk settles down over the city, and, there like you knew—you've been waiting as well, haven't you?—there's the park. The only park. The right park.

Stay at the curb for ten minutes, for twenty minutes, your hands curled over the steering wheel, like if you let the steering wheel go this image will fade, this memory will get sucked back into the past.

But it's real.

You lead Thomas out into it, the seed pods crackling under his feet in a way that makes him lift his feet high, smile.

Hold his hand. Remember.

Look across, through the equipment, for a woman sitting on a bench, oblivious.

She's not there.

Just, standing by the tree, her shoulders shaking, a younger woman, her boyfriend or husband trying to console her, each of them with hair the color of straw, with faces washed even lighter.

Distraught, that's the word.

Two people come back to the playground at night, the same way ghouls traipse out into a cemetery under the moonlight?

Wait, see.

Thomas slips away from your hand, rushes out to the jungle gym, the swings, the slide, and the woman looks up to him like she's waking from a dream. And then she looks across the playground, for this boy's watcher.

Only—it's your instincts.

Of course you've stood such that the wide tree trunk is directly behind you. Of course you've stood such that you fade, that she doesn't see you. Such that this perfect little boy, he's running out of nowhere, and from no one.

Her hands stabs down, takes her boyfriend's, her husband's. She makes him look.

At Thomas.

He's climbing the slide, the one with the plastic hood at the top.

Look ahead of him, to the jacket in the crow's nest, whipping in the light wind.

Smile, bite your lower lip in.

An instant later, your chest hollowing out with fear, Thomas ducks into the red plastic hood, that brief and forever tunnel, and when he slides out, the metal beneath him polished by a hundred thousand years of human existence, the hood amplifies his scream of delight.

His voice.

The woman rushes out to him, collects him from the woodchips and holds him close, like a package she's stealing, her left hand cradling the back of his head, and then she looks around one more time, for you, but you're in the shadows now, your head moving back and forth in something like a dry heave, something like joy, enough that you have to cover your mouth to keep it in, and like that you let Thomas go, let him have the life he deserves, the life you always wanted for him, and whether you go back to your old ways or just keep fading, it doesn't matter.

Things are already in motion. Like they always have been.

Thank you. From all of us.

STORY NOTES

Interstate Love Affair

I distinctly remember pulling over to the side of the road out by Shallowater, Texas one day and getting most of the way in the ditch so I could write down the first sentence or two of this story. Like it had just drifted in through the side glass. And then, after scratching down those few words, about a hundred yards down the road there was this big old mangy dog running in the ditch. So I stopped, went out into the cotton fields, chased him down, cornered him some lucky how, carried him back to the cab of my truck and closed the door gently, so as not to spook him. Then I got in behind the wheel, to take us on what I was sure was going to be the first of our many adventures. Except he kept coming across the bench seat and biting me on the arm and the side and the shoulder. So, after about four miles of that I had to pull over again, dive out my side so that dog could explode out past me, go on with whatever his plans had been for that day, before I delivered him far off course. Then, hunting a month or so later with one of my cousins, who's into medicine, I kept asking him all these oblique, kind of sidelong questions about, you know, like, what if somebody had rabies, say, and they didn't want to have it anymore, like, what would ~~this hypothetical person~~ this *character* I was writing maybe do about that whole situation? And, that walk through the trees when I was just completely camouflaging my real intentions, this snowstorm was blowing in hard and blinding, and we weren't dressed even close for it, but we were Blackfeet, on Blackfeet land, so we weren't so nervous. Just step, squint, lean into the wind; wash rinse repeat, until some kind of blue light just fizzed into existence right over our heads, enough to cast our shadows in the wrong directions, bright enough that we ducked, didn't know what was happening, didn't know what *could* be happening. And then a few steps later we kind of felt something, and looked back into Glacier Park, to one of those big rock faces that reach into the sky higher than Tolkien ever dreamed, and this snowy face of it that must have been the size of Rhode Island, it just calved off, fell in slow motion, so far away. And that's related to this, for me. That massiveness. Our smallness in comparison. That combination of mystery and fear that adds up to awe, if you can just not look away. But, that Deridder-lift that gets things going: I'd recently studied that from every angle I had access to, and still couldn't decide if it was some animal not on the books or if it was just hype. The way my heart was pounding, though, it was real real real. I wanted to go there, lick the asphalt where that animal had been found. So, William, for me, he was how I charted the distance between 'cryptid' and 'Pomeranian.' Also involved, I guess, was I'd had to bail one of my dogs out from the pound in Lubbock not long before. The tech walked me back to this one black dog they had that didn't really fit the description I'd given, but what the heck, and sure enough it was her, and her intestines had all fallen out, were hanging down in the newly-loose skin of her left leg, and her front paw was just a skeleton hand she was holding up because it wouldn't take weight anymore, and she was mostly burn and blood and starvation, and the tech kind of eeked his mouth out, said Why hadn't the driver just put her down already? I kind of wondered that too. She should have died in the road. Except she had to come home. We were her people. And, because there was nowhere to hold her that didn't make her cry out, she had to drag herself out to the truck, get up into it herself. And it was a tall truck. And she made it through those next few weeks, her whole body white with gauze, then she limped through the next eight years, and finally only died up here in Colorado, after many more injuries (she cut her neck way too open once, she had some teeth knocked out with a bat, she got chewed by other dogs, but still, I'd trade any ten dogs just to have her again. Any ten dogs and most people). So this story, it's about dogs, yeah. I think most of my stories are, really. Dog and trucks, and fathers, all in some narrative petri dish, just add antifreeze and radiation, let cook overnight. But, the more macro why of this story: I'd told somebody once, and said it like I knew what I was talking about, that we should all, at least once, write the thing we're most scared of. For me, that's always been a person with a dog head. My single biggest fear is walking around some corner and into the chest of some solid dude, then looking up, and up, and seeing this Anubis kind of head just starting to tilt down, apprehend this disturbance. It still terrifies me. I thought I could exorcise it with this story, but, man this story just made it so much worse. I wrote it in like three days, I think, and loved it, thought it was perfect, but it wouldn't let go of me the way most stories will, or know to do. So then I wrote forty or fifty thousand more words of it, turned it into this big violent novel, hoping to get rid of that image. It was an effort that cost me nearly twenty pounds, too. Every time I sat down to write it, to back my way into this particularly dark space, that dog-head guy would stand up just behind me and I couldn't turn around, couldn't even think how to, so I'd gag, not be able to eat for that whole day. But I couldn't let go of the keyboard, either, knew that the only way out was by writing. That's always the only real way out. So I tried, and I tried, and it completely didn't work, if what chasing that novel down was supposed to do was make me not scared of dog-headed people. Really, it just gave them names, and trucks. But, anyway, this piece that's here, it's the front of that novel. And very much involved with it is how much I always hated getting ticks and ringworms and lice in elementary school. Well, not the lice so much, who cares about lice, but I always hated having a tick on me, latched deep, and always felt like my revulsion was a very specific kind, that I was feeling it deeper than anybody else who was having a tick on them. And, yeah, the title's completely an STP-steal; that's one of my favorite of all songs. And, as for why Tomball, it's that the whole Houston area's always freaked me out. It's so hot and humid and muggy, and there's so many people, and they're all doing all these things I can't even guess at, and for reasons I'll never know. But I can't write about the city, I never really understand cities, so I wrote about out where one of my good friends lives, because the pastures out that direction, I kind of recognize them. They feel real to me in a way that I can do them on the page. And, I-10 there: I've driven ruts in that road, I think, going back and forth from Texas to Florida. You get a lot of ideas, late at night. And sometimes they turn into stories, and you think you can vomit them up through your fingertips, be done with it, have it gone for good. But there's always more.

No Takebacks

That elegance you're always looking for with code? How some red-eyed night you might sneak up on a recursive statement that can make a page or two not matter anymore? How you can luck your way into a simple string_replace trick or a way of passing variables nobody's thought of yet, but that everybody should have been thinking of all along? That's exactly the same elegance you're looking for with fiction. Or, that's exactly the same elegance I'm always looking for, anyway. I'll stay awake however long it takes to luck onto it. I'll do the piece over and over, trying every which way, even ways I know are going to be broke, just on the chance that the right way'll be shadowing me as I work. And that I can turn my head fast enough to see it. Problem is, I don't have nearly enough elegance to try to program *and* write fiction, at least not anymore. Or maybe it's a patience-thing, or maybe I'm just not smart enough to manage both. Or maybe I've just had too many concussions, finally. But I still remember that hazy joy of being awake for three days, peeling through pages of not-really-that-natural syntax, and how it can all be worth it with one magic RETURN. This story comes directly from that. I'd done it once before, with this story that turned up in *Asimov's*, but this story took a dark turn just a whole lot faster. It completely surprised me, too. I went in thinking it was going to be a couple thousand words and done, go see a movie now, you earned that torn stub, but it kept scaring me more and more, and there kept being more layers under the one I thought had already been the last one. That last scene? It still terrifies me. Of everything I've written, it's been the stickiest, at least for me. But I guess that's just because, like Eli Roth says, the best horror, it's personal. Which is to say, the horror that works best on me, the horror I can make the most real, it's the horror that just bleeds up through my pores. That's in my DNA deeper than I can ever get at with anything but story. So. That morning before the afternoon I wrote this story, my wife and I'd hit a garage sale, and she'd bought this huge ancient-old surely-haunted lamp, then put it in the back of our truck such that, every time I checked the rearview, there was that lampshade, sneaking up on me. It was spectacularly creepy. But—it was like this deer head I grew up with, that my granddad I never met had shot before I was born. That deer stalked my whole childhood. It got to where I couldn't sleep if that deer wasn't on the wall in my room, so I could watch it, keep it from stepping out of the wall. I dreamed about it so many nights, and then, one night, I woke from a nightmare of that deer and it was in bed with me, had fallen off the wall. That was a bad night. And now this lamp, it was my deer, just all at once, some kind of childhood-horror transfer-ence that I'd stupidly assumed I could be immune to. If I could see that lamp in the rearview, then that meant I knew where it was, at least. And that was far better than the alternative. So, as these things go, I came home, wrote this story after lunch, just all at once, like a backcountry amputation, and still had to sneak upstairs when I was done. And that sneaking-upstairs, it was way more complicated than usual that night, because light, that's supposed to be what saves you, right? Except now it was lamps I was terrified of. And then, to make it all worse, for some reason we put that lamp in the landing outside our bedroom door, so, some nights I'll still wake up, kind of look out there, and there's that lamp, just standing there. Waiting. I hate that lamp. In the nighttime, at least. In daytime, it's pretty all right. But so's the deer. And, as for the dog stuffed with jewelry, I think that's from a trip to the vet with a sick dog. She'd been eating rocks, and was looking pretty dead on her feet, and I got to talking to the vet about all the weird things she's had to cut-and-forceps out of dogs. And there was some pretty insane stuff, and I couldn't seem to stop thinking about it all. And about what if she only *thought* the dogs had been eating all that on their own. And, that scene early on, where they're hanging in the kitchen and the dad comes in, for some reason that feels like one of the most real things I've ever written. I'm not good at just a whole lot of stuff, I don't think, but I can do sixteen years old like nobody's business. No clue why, really. Once Will Christopher Baer said to me that I really had this teen-angst thing all the way down, man. I left thinking yeah, he sees it, he knows, dude's got an eye. Except then I got to thinking that maybe that wasn't so much of a compliment. But I can still take it that way, if I squint right. And, as for the title, it's just—we *don't* get any takebacks, right? And I think that's good. The world would be all messed up if we did. One of my favorite stories, RM Berry's "Metempsychosis," that first bit's always haunted me: "Dougherty dreams of second chances. He doesn't feel cheated so much as simply baffled by irreversibility. Things happen. They don't happen again." For all of my life, I've been right there with Dougherty. And many thanks to Laird Barron for picking this one up for the debut issue of *Phantasmagorium*. I like to think Laird's one of the smarter people I know—and I know he's one of the best writers writing—so, that he ran it, it means a lot.

The Coming of Night

I started this one completely meaning to write a choose-your-own-adventure story. Except then I realized that, if this guy's the killer he thinks he is, then there's not really any choice, is there? Of course not. For other, weaker people, maybe. But not for him. For him there's only ever one bright shining path, and he's most definitely walking it, never needing to look to either side, or behind. I wrote this one very spur-of-the-moment, too, kind of as a test: I was teaching an on-line workshop for *LitReactor*, and figured the best way to show how to write a story is to just maybe write a story, let the class watch it happen scene-by-scene. Which is so much more difficult than I'd suspected, especially when people start chiming in after each new bit, *especially* this one student Derek Palmer, who's a dangerously intuitive reader, the kind it's hard to ever get ahead of. Those kinds of readers, though, they make you better. But still, that 'test'-part: I figured if I was any kind of halfway real writer, then this was a thing I should be able to get done. And so I did. The only way to go into things is with nerve, right? But you can fake it, too. I always fake it. I opened my notebook pretty much at random and pointed to a story premise: *kill a guy, find leathery eggs in his gut. take those eggs home. incubate them?* That was all I had to go on, and that first public session, I probably crossed two-thousand words or so. Which isn't much. But for me it was some distance, since it was largely in a bar, and I don't know the first thing about bars. The real meat, for me, though, it was getting that first vic back to the hotel room, then getting down to the sharp-edged part of the night. I love writing that kind of stuff. Really, I've got this other novel, this way violent thing, that's pretty much just that, over and over. Some days you want to see how far you can go, right? And maybe peer over into where you definitely shouldn't go. And then sneak across anyway. But this guy, man, he's one of my all-time favorite characters. I love his efficiency, his sense of purpose. And, those eggs, they about killed me. I had no idea what was going to be in them, where they were from, what they were for, and I wasn't real sure I was going to have the nerve to figure it out. Even the fake nerve. This is one of those stories where I kept writing dead ends and having to backtrack

(<u>publicly</u>). As for where they're from, those eggs, it's something I read in . . . maybe Harry Crews' *Childhood*? Or maybe some Dorothy Allison? Except those are all seeming halfway wrong—right part of the country, wrong writers. Anyway, somewhere I read that a turtle egg, no matter how long you boil it, the shell either will or won't go soft. Or hard. It won't go the opposite of whatever it is in the first place. And that just confuses me. I mean, I guess it means that turtle eggs, they don't act like other eggs. And I can't figure why. And I have no real idea how other eggs act, either, but still, turtle eggs, they're not like those other, boring eggs. Which makes them so, so interesting to me. And, I think I wrote this story after seeing a bunch of turtle heads popping up in the ocean down off Baja California, right about sunset. I thought they were seals at first, but they were turtles, just periscoping up to see if this was a good place to come lay some eggs. I guess. Or maybe they were waiting for me to go to sleep, so they could come gnaw my throat open, I don't know. Of all the animals, turtles are forever the most scary to me. My great-grandfather, when I was young he told me that, if a turtle ever bit me, then it wouldn't let go until it thundered. So I grew up being absolutely terrified of turtles. I remember once finding one eating a rat head, and just knowing that rat head was what was left of me, that I was sneaking an accidental peek into the someday future. Another time I got hopelessly marooned out on a rock in a creek, because I thought I saw a turtle. So, anything that comes from a turtle, and possibly holds more turtles, for me that thing's going to automatically have a high creep factor. Used to, as kind of a ward, I had this page I'd photocopied up from some architecture memoir anthology or something—it was this one architect's childhood drawings of turtles. Just in margins, on envelopes, wherever. Like they were in him, and were always going to be leaking out through his pencil. But then one day one of his teachers told him turtles were stupid, he needed to stop drawing turtles, and—this is the horror part of this—*he listened to her*. After that, he never drew another turtle, and finally drifted into a successful career in architecture. I kind of felt like, hanging that photocopy up, it told turtles that we were good, that it was all all right. That I understood. But I don't. Also related to all this, I guess, is that I've never even once driven by a turtle in the road without circling back, carrying it to the ditch it's pointing at in its slow, deliberate way. And sometimes I end up sitting there after, to be sure that was really the way that turtle meant to be going. I have no human feeling for those people who steer over, to clip turtles, flip them across the other lane like a tiddlywink. I've found those turtles, bloody and cracked, so confused that their one defense wasn't enough, when it always had been. And I've walked those turtles to the fence, pulled the necessary dirt over them, and lowered my head in apology. Just for being human. And, those strange-nosed folk in this story, who I kind of saw as angels: they're completely a graft from *Star Trek: The Next Generation*. The Traveler's species. That guy always fascinates me. Whenever I have downtime, I often find myself thinking of him. The original title for this story was "Little Stealers," too. I think it was ramping off that Bradbury story "The Small Assassin." But I can't imagine why this story would ever have been called "Little Stealers." That must have been some dead-end I ran down, backed out of. Also I should cite this one Charles Beaumont story, "The Howling Man," from (for me) Ann and Jeff VanderMeer's *The Weird*. It's kind of just a joke of a story, but the lightness of the delivery, this kind of over-constructed indirectness, this mid-twentieth-century casual 'worldliness,' it kept making me think it was on purpose, that it was told like that because it was trying to hide something far,

far darker, something that was still going to be there after the punchline. Something Beaumont had *seen*, and been a part of. And this was as close as he could come to documenting it, as warning for the rest of us. It's one of the main things stories are for, isn't it? We shouldn't let ourselves forget. And, the ending for this one, it took a lot of tries. About a week's worth of them, hammering away every afternoon. Which is way unusual for me, as far as short stuff goes. But this one, I couldn't let it go, I couldn't throw it away. Most of my horror stories, they leave me kind of weirded out, like, I know this is one of those nights I'm not turning the light off. But this one, it hit me a lot deeper, in a much more vital place. Just reduced me to nothing, erased me. Hopefully it touches you a little bit wrong as well.

ACKNOWLEDGMENTS

Three Miles Past never would have happened if Mark Scioneaux hadn't flagged me over to his table at World Horror in Salt Lake City in 2011. He showed me what Nightscape was about. By then I'd already been talking to Robert Shane Wilson for a while, about that excellent *Horror for Good* anthology, which I loserly never got around to actually sending a story across for. But what Mark wondered was if I had any novellas they could maybe run. My first thought was that I had no idea what a novella was, or how it worked. My next thought was that it's just a long story, right? Just one not so long as a novel? I shot four across to him, finally. And, instead of taking one, he said maybe they could just take them all; the other's "Sterling City," coming out all by itself. So, yes, cons are where good things happen, sometimes. And, as for the original Nightscape Press edition cover, by Boden Steiner—I know Boden from around Denver, and have always dug his work. So, when we needed a cover, I was begging for Boden to work on it. What he also did, though, was title the book. Since this wasn't a collection until Mark and Robert suggested it, I hadn't ever thought on what a title for it could be. As close as I could come was Gertrude Stein's *Three Lives*. But what does Stein have to do with horror, right? I just shot all three stories to Boden as single files, told him I didn't even have an order for them yet. And then he came back with that title—a lift from the first story. And it completely works. So, thanks for the art and the title, Boden, and thanks to Mark for flagging me down, and, thanks to Robert for cleaning the stories up for me so much. Other people to thank: Stephen King, for all his 'haunted object' stories (word processors, laundry presses, etc.), each of which always gets to me; this dog I saw just at the edge of my headlights one night lost in the mountains of New Mexico, a dog who was standing there holding what I'll swear was a human forearm and hand in its mouth; John Langan, who, with his fiction, challenged me to write one of these; Nick Kimbro, for talking horror and horror and horror, always, and writing it, too; Matthew Treon, for not-on-purposely showing me a last-minute fix for the first story; Joe R. Lansdale, for always setting the standard for horror stories, and just for how to be a writer *and* a person; and, to my wife Nancy: the one dream I've ever had about being really and actually dead, I wasn't, because you were there with me. We were nineteen again, holding hands, moving so fast down a blacktop road in Texas that we had to be ghosts. It didn't matter, though. We were together. Thank you for that, and for all of this.

ABOUT THE AUTHOR

Stephen Graham Jones is the *New York Times*-bestselling author of more than forty novels, collections, novellas, and comic books, including *The Only Good Indians* and the Indian Lake Trilogy. Jones received a National Endowment for the Arts fellowship and has won honors ranging from the Mark Twain American Voice in Literature Award to the Bram Stoker Award. Jones lives and teaches in Boulder, Colorado. Visit his website at stephengrahamjones.com.

STEPHEN GRAHAM JONES

FROM OPEN ROAD MEDIA

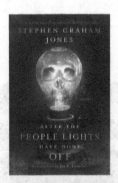

INTEGRATED MEDIA

INTEGRATED MEDIA